For Bryce, a space oddity gone too soon.

PRAISE FOR *NECRONAUTS*

"I loved this novel for the ways it captured a small town through obituaries (obits unlike those published in any small-town newspaper because they are obituaries of revelations, of story, not a listing of facts). And then those obituaries work in conversation with vintage photos that hang over the stories spectrally. This novel is a gritty, elegiac fever dream of the American West that explores the strange intersections of belief, addiction, and masculinity."

Grant Faulkner, author of *All the Comfort Sin Can Provide*

"Ryan Habermeyer makes of Calypsee, Utah a kind of Winesburg of the West, inhabited by doomed and lonely believers. Necronauts is obsessed with death but brimming with vivid and excessive life, strange but credible. The book is a marvel of form and voice, its effects far more glorious than gloomy."

Chris Bachelder, author of *Dayswork* and *The Throwback Special*

"*Necronauts* is something special: a novel in miniatures whose concerns are so large it feels almost cosmic. If you were to trace its family tree looking for ancestors, you might find *Invisible Cities* along one branch and *Spoon River Anthology* along another, with W. G. Sebald and Jeff VanderMeer among its nearby cousins. Ultimately, though, it's a book that transcends its heritage. Through its strange, barbed, wistful catalogue of uncanny recovered obituaries, it introduces us to a town full of people who, as the author might put it, "feel the holes in their hearts swallowing their hearts." So, I confess, do I. And so, I bet, do you."

Kevin Brockmeier, author of *The Ghost Variations*

Necronauts: A Novel

Written by
Mark Habermeyer

Edited By
Ryan Habermeyer

FIRST EDITION

All inquiries may be directed to

Stillhouse Press
4400 University Drive, 3E4
Fairfax, VA 22030
www.stillhousepress.org

Stillhouse Press is an independent, student- and alumni-run nonprofit press based out of Northern Virginia and operated in collaboration with Watershed Lit: Center for Literary Engagement and Publishing Practice at George Mason University.

LCCN: 2025947567

ISBN-13: 978-1-945233-32-6

EPUB ISBN: 978-1-945233-32-7

Jacket Design: Camille Koslo

Interior Design: Paul Logan IV

Here I could pluck the stars
with my hand. I dare not speak aloud
in the silence. For fear
of disturbing the dwellers of heaven.

—Li Bai, "Written on a Wall at Summit-Top Temple"

"He picked up a sharp ax to remove the bark and the rough surface. But just as he was about to deliver the first blow, he heard a small voice say, 'Don't strike me hard.' He turned his terrified eyes all around the room to discover from where the little voice could possibly have come, but he saw nobody! He looked under the bench—nobody. He looked into a cupboard that was always shut—nobody. He looked into a basket of shavings and sawdust—nobody. He even opened the door of the shop and glanced into the street—and still nobody. Who, then, could it be?"

—Carlo Collodi, *Pinocchio*

"There is no God, only Cosmos. We are at the will of and controlled by Cosmos. There is no absolute will—we are marionettes, mechanical puppets, machines, movie characters."

—Konstantin Tsiolkovsky

Editor's Note

Calypsee is just off old Highway 21 on the northern fringe of Utah's Escalante Desert. It rarely appears on maps. It was founded by nine polygamist families of Swedes and Germans in 1857, sent by Brigham Young to mine silver. They found pitchblende instead and up until the Manhattan Project the locals manufactured a mildly radioactive green glass that is now a collector's item, but historically it was known as a spa town where asthmatics traveled to bathe in uranium water. It's all RV parks, golf courses, and little Mormon chapels now. The graveyard is quite full. As of last week, my father is buried there.

We had not spoken in many years. Most of our conversations circled around the weather, or baseball, or the photographs he'd taken of Bigfoot in Cache Valley which were conveniently blurry. We didn't have much to say, neither of us living up to the imagination of the other. My parents divorced when I was in diapers, and because my mother rarely let me visit except for a few fishing trips, I never knew my father, or this town which was his one true mistress, until I started packing up the attic after the funeral.

My son, who never met his grandfather, played in the yard while I sorted through mildewed boxes of UFO reports and old cassettes of Art Bell's Coast to Coast program dating back to the eighties. You got to believe in something, my father used to say, even if it's wrong—just believe. Maybe that's what kept him alive in his old age. His own father had disowned him after he converted to Mormonism in his twenties, warning my father not to go west, that Utah is a drug, a crazed saint's playground both hated and hating, an apple that tastes like an onion but looks like a grape, warning him that once there he'd never leave. I don't think my father could ever figure out if he was one of the Mormons or not. He ran for mayor once on the slogan BRING BACK DESERET NATION, but even this wouldn't endear him to the locals. He lost in a landslide. He built bombs at Thiokol, sang in the choir, took Boy Scouts on camping trips, and wrote a weekly column in the town newspaper, but he could never be one of them. He could never be a true-believing Mormon of pioneer stock. That's something you're born with, something in the blood. I think it was that alienation, not an aneurysm, that killed him in the end.

Among the knickknacks were the yellowed pages of every article my father had ever written for the local newspaper, pinned to the walls of the house. While my son played in the yard with the neighbor's kid, the two of them in dresses and pretending the cardboard boxes over their heads were space helmets, I sorted through a vast collection of obituaries in the bathroom. Almost all of them were from 1985 or thereabouts, the year my mother left him, the year I started to believe God was a novice puppeteer fumbling the strings as he tangled our lives with deranged glee. He didn't just write the obituaries but visited their graves, scrubbing the tombstones with a toothbrush and bringing flowers. *The living and the dead are castaways in the same shipwreck,* my father wrote. *They are alive in us, and we are dead in them.* Of the nearly thousand and one original obituaries plastered to the bathroom walls I've curated ninety-five here, ones I think my father liked best if his greasy thumbprints smearing the ink is any proof. I omitted names out of privacy for the deceased and included several photographs I can only assume my father took, lightly revising a few details I found unbelievable because fathers create their sons but in the end it's sons who invent their fathers.

When John Steinbeck passed through town on his great American road trip, Calypsee was little more than a footnote in his imagination. The librarian told him the town name was either short for apocalypse or in honor of the Greek nymph Calypso because there were plenty of them. Nymphs or catastrophes? Steinbeck wondered. What's the difference? the librarian said. Steinbeck wrote to his second wife that Calypsee was "the damned prettiest sight outside of Monterrey," and "if you shot every sonfabitch Mormon, well, then I'd even call it heaven." On postcards he sent to friends he called it a quiet town where nobody is a foreigner, nobody is sick, nobody is ignored, a town of misfits, perverts, and prophets all addicted to religion, but the whores are well-behaved and the water supply is fluorinated twice a day. He called it a landfill, a hymn, a detour, a blot of ink on an outdated map, a cabinet not cleaned of its cobwebs for many years, an ecstasy, a bile, a rapture, a windswept place where time stretches like taffy reminding us the world is spinning a little too fast, a place where dreams go to take a nap.

Steinbeck wasn't right. But he wasn't wrong either. In Utah, every story you hear is true. It just depends what kind of truth you're looking for. That's why it's easy to get lost in the desert. Every road is an illusion. My advice is if you're looking for Calypsee you won't find it in these pages, the graveyard of my father's mind. Head west and keep driving until you get behind a pickup truck with a bumper sticker that says IN ARMAGEDDON WE TRUST. Then you know you're almost home.

—R.M. Habermeyer
Salt Lake City
March 2020

I Am a Traveler of Both Time and Space

It is with sadness we communicate the passing of the woodcutter who reminds us that to die in Utah is a house-keeping concern. Our pioneer ancestors understood this. They welcomed summer passings, knowing under conditions of such salty, dry heat the soul is quick to breach its housing contract as the body shrivels into dust. But death in winter is precarious. Especially in the desert where temperatures are savage and this world touches another. A century ago, winter corpses waiting for the ground to thaw and left outdoors were easily dragged off by wild animals, while those kept in an attic or spare room for safekeeping often forgot they were dead and wandered about the house prone to mischief. Such was the dilemma our town faced many years ago when burying the wood-cutter's boy claimed by the typhoid epidemic. The mayor had placed a moratorium on burials on account of the ice storm which rendered all grave-digging equipment inoper-able. But the woodcutter, son of a carpenter with mustard gas still rattling in his lungs, would not be dissuaded. He consulted the town charter which indicated in the event of inclement weather the bereaved may petition the local bishop for a stick of dynamite and a shovel. Who can forget the excellent blast it produced in the frozen earth? True, the cemetery caretaker had forgotten to move the coffin, the dynamite scattering the poor boy's remains into the sky, but Germans exiled in the desert turn remarkably optimistic, catastrophe being the curious balm of faith. The woodcutter rallied the congregation into a scavenger hunt to collect the missing pieces of his son, which in the years since has evolved into the annual spring festival where neighbors emerge from domestic hibernation and exchange Jell-O squares. A year after his catastrophe, the woodcutter opened a crematorium downtown hoping to spare others his misfortune. While the faithful considered it an abomination, nobody could deny the ingenuity of the woodcutter who pioneered peephole windows on all the furnace ovens so grieving family members could watch the process. The crematorium closed a few months ago after decades of mismanagement, and the property has been promptly renovated into a pizzeria. The grand opening was a success. On cold nights we often walk past the old family building. Hypnotized by the neon lights, we follow a perfume of basil and marinara into the alley and peer through window slits to eavesdrop on neighbors, but mostly to admire the wisps of smoke billowing from the ovens, leaning against the brick walls whose warmth offers a strange, silent relief.

Let the Sun Beat Down Upon

It is with sadness we communicate the passing of the acclaimed rodeo clown. His estranged son, given up for adoption as a child, found him yesterday and remains visibly shaken. Father and son had, it seems, after many years of cautious communication, finally agreed to meet at the hotel. The son knew very little about his father, only that he was the youngest child of a master clown famous in Moldovan carnivals. Those who have seen the blurry photographs say the son's grandfather sits in a chair surrounded by his nine sons, their faces painted and expressionless, making it impossible for anyone to know which of them is the son's father. Not long after the photograph was taken, the grandfather banished his son from the community for teaching the clandestine—and now extinct— clown language to a woman from a non-clowning family. The two married and fled to America. The son found his father drowned in the hotel bathtub. His face was painted in the customary Tramp style. Worried someone might think poorly of him in that condition, the son tried in vain to clean his father's face, only to discover what he believed was clown makeup was actually the old man's real skin. His father had spent a lifetime applying paints and powders and resins when he was not performing to mask his natural clown face.

Stars to Fill My Dreams

It is with sadness we communicate the passing of the chef who died after a brief illness. Many of us were lucky to forage with her, scouring under mesquite as we nibbled here and there on wild mushroom breeds. She showed us how to find them at night, their caps poking through the soil and peering over the grass like shy UFOs. She knew which mushrooms caused drowsiness, or euphoria, or hallucinations. She knew how to squeeze them just right until they leaked an eerie green bioluminescence. Luciferin, she called it. Like the devil, Lucifer, the light bringer gone stray. At the library, she showed us an old medieval book on display under thick glass. Each page beautifully ornamented with letters and pictures. There's a mushroom, she said, almost translucent as glass. Once picked it dissolves into a black juice monks used for ink. *Morchella relicta*. The weeping mushrooms of immortality. A silly name, the chef laughed, but warned the ink was corrosive. As it aged it sunk into the manuscript paper and soaked the fibers, spreading until the whole page stained black. Entire libraries were lost like this. Some of the books were burned to prevent the contamination, others clasped shut and hidden deep in monasteries. Who knows how many other books are out there written in this strange ink, she used to tell us, waiting for someone to open them, for the ink to run off the page, the words spilling down the streets in a black river of calligraphy.

To Be Where I Have Been

It is with sadness we communicate the passing of the local librarian. Many will recall with fondness her campaigns against what she called the other great Satan, the Oxford English Dictionary, and its subsidiaries. Every year she sent a cease-and-desist letter to the famed university, demanding they alter the history of the Oxford comma which, according to her calculations, her family had invented, and every year her lawsuit seeking royalties for its usage were promptly dismissed in court. She was from Russia. During the war she spied for the Cheka as a prostitute, code name *Bomba*. She fired a bazooka. She ate mice at Stalingrad. She buried four children. Following the war, she stayed briefly with her husband, a butcher, but he would rather talk Plato with customers than grind sausage. He hanged himself. Upon arriving in Utah, she quickly filled the post of librarian due to her impeccable command of the language. She never wore nylons. She refused to be photographed, saying the camera steals your soul. She liked to stand in doorways and smoke cigarettes. She told men her code name but nobody believed her. For companionship she wrote poetry. In one, a mother in a city under siege befriends some orphans and they spend the afternoon playing baseball with a live grenade. In another, a woman gets apples with her weekly rations but when she returns home, they are the heads of the babies she's miscarried. She files a complaint with the civil supply office and is placed under surveillance. None of these were published. Shortly after the Sputnik launch, she wrote a poem where a widow finds her dead husband's balalaikas in a closet. When she plays it, the spirit of Josef Stalin appears. First, she toys with little Koba. She shaves his mustache and makes him dance the Kamarinskaya. She reads erotic letters written to him by Roosevelt. Rather than have him judged by a military tribunal, the widow forces Stalin to perform tedious housework: scrub toilets, iron clothes, beat the dust out of rugs, and fetch vegetables from the market. With each task, Stalin's spirit fades a little. The poem ends with the widow putting on Stalin's decorated military uniform, memorizing paragraphs from the Communist Manifesto, and becoming a Stalin impersonator wandering the streets of Salt Lake City. The librarian died at her desk. A letter with fat Cyrillic letters was found in her pocket. As far as anyone can tell, the letter says how an immigration officer reviewing her visa had changed her name on the official documents from the Cyrillic to Roman alphabet. You can't make these little marks on a typewriter, he told her, pointing to the diacritics, they don't exist in English. I've devoted my entire life to words, she scribbled in her spidery cursive handwriting, so what do you do when you've worked decades to hold onto your pain only to have it stolen by a typewriter?

Just Say Nobody

It is with sadness we communicate the passing of the former cantaloupe queen who died after too heartily consuming the fruit that made her a beloved fixture in our town. All are invited to her funeral. Except the dentist—a man with the personality of a diaper rash—who discovered her body and while waiting for the authorities to arrive went snooping inside the old missile silo the deceased had converted into a Bed & Breakfast and found the cosmonaut boy hiding inside a vintage baby blue Frigidaire, the same boy who had crawled through the skylight of the dentist's office a month earlier and trashed the place after bumping three vials of ketamine. Kolob, the kids nicknamed it, because the drug makes you feel like a star in outer space. The boy crawled out of the Frigidaire slowly, the heavy space helmet drooping to one side as the dentist told him he couldn't sleep here. The boy made some signs with his hands and the dentist shook his head saying, Sorry kid, I don't speak alien. The boy made the same signs again, as if saying he had nowhere else to go. You're the kid who believes he's an alien, the dentist said. Jesus, what are you some kind of retard? Most days, the cosmonaut boy's fingers seemed to say as the two of them crawled out of the bunker, I feel like a lone raindrop heavy in the white mute sky. He followed the dentist home and stood quietly outside the window. Later, he stood in his underwear as the dentist ran a bath and rubbed lotions on the thick pink scales in the creases of his arms and the bends of his knees, and the dentist said he looked like a tree that fucked a piglet. I don't blame you for wanting to get rid of this skin, he said, it's a goddamn Halloween costume for sure. The boy moved his fingers. The dentist said, You know you're not really an alien, right? The boy's fingers moved fast, almost like they were saying the Mormons wouldn't let him go home. He didn't flinch when the dentist rubbed disinfectant on the blown-out veins on his feet. The dentist sat on the toilet and pulled up the sleeves on the dirty linen jacket he always wore, the one with the yellowed pocket square. He soaked it each morning in a mixture of nitrous, paint thinner, and Special K. A whippit, he called it. He asked the cosmonaut boy for his name and watched the boy's fingers move again, then he sorted through the boy's Army-issued duffle bag that included hypodermic needles, cassette tapes, a photo of his mother, a smoke-spackled light bulb, old sci-fi VHS tapes, a broken parabolic microphone, a scuffed baseball, and a dog-eared library copy of the poems of Li Bai. Despite the dentist telling the boy he couldn't stay, the boy's fingers kept moving as if saying, I'm nobody from nowhere. You talk too much, the dentist said, as the boy's space helmet rocked back and forth and his fingers only stopped moving after the dentist fixed him a bump of ketamine. The Bed & Breakfast is under new management. Rooms are twelve dollars per night. Laundry not included.

Nobody knew why he wore the space helmet. It wasn't a cheap plastic toy, or prop from Battle Beyond the Sun, *but a thick globe two sizes too big for his head, the glass mottled and white like a soap-scummed fishbowl he'd stolen from the pet shop. Nobody knew what his face looked like. He kept the visor pulled down. He never took it off. Like he was waiting to be abducted. We said he'd been in an accident during a fallout drill in school. We said he was sick. We said he was touching himself in the girls' bathroom at church and God cursed him. We said he was a Russian spy. Nobody knew for sure.*

Nobody knew if the space helmet latched onto a metallic corselet and neck ring that seemed to be sutured to his collarbones was a medical experiment gone wrong or something else. There was a small bullet hole on the helmet's left side where his cheek would have been. Milky cracks radiated from the hole like spider webs. Nobody knew if he'd been shot or shot himself.

Nobody was born with a space helmet. We said this to make ourselves feel better. We said this because he was a freak, a sin, a loser, a retard. We believed it. We have to believe it.

Nobody was surprised when he spent all his time at the local theatre watching too many campy sci-fi movies and they made him go brainbroke, believing he was an alien forgotten by the mothership. Nobody tried to convince the Mormons he would be their missionary and bring news of their faith to the cosmos if only he could use their satellites, but nobody believed him.

Nobody knew if he could hear us. Sometimes it sounded like he was trying to say something. We took the oxygen hose serpentining from the back of the helmet and held it to our ears. We heard murmurs. We heard static and radio feedback loop. Nobody knew what he was saying. We guessed. He spoke with his fingers. Nobody bothered to learn sign language.

Nobody remembered when he was born. It was like he'd always been part of the town. Our ghost. The canker in our mouths we licked hoping it would go away but never did. He'd been in and out of foster care and halfway houses. Nobody wanted him.

All my life has been a head full of stars, his fingers seemed to say. Nobody believed it.

Nobody knew his name. So, we called him Nobody.

Hic Occultus Occulto Occisus Est

It is with sadness we communicate the passing of the stamp collector, an aged brother in Christ who died peacefully in his shop last Monday. His funeral was poorly attended. For more than half a century he was a regular fixture in the mottled window downtown hunched over his albums with a pair of tweezers as he dutifully licked stamps. As a boy he had an insatiable tongue. Always licking things, his mother complained. Spoons, doorknobs, wallpaper. His mother bought him stamps to prevent him from licking girls and other disagreeable things. He rented a little shop next to the post office and anyone mailing a letter had him lick the envelope shut along with the stamp for a small fee. Even after the switch to self-adhesive stamps people in town preferred his tongue. By the time he was a teen-ager he had amassed quite a collection. Stamps with birds, railroads, ships, castles, bald men. Stamps from extinct nations like Prussia and Tibet, and of course Nazi stamps which he said were everybody's favorite. He spent all his life searching for the elusive 1849 Mormon stamp with Brigham Young's face superimposed over a beehive with the words DESERET. But it was never about the collecting. He liked the taste of old stamps. The ones left to yellow in attics, with creases and tears and oily finger residue. They tasted like a desert with tangy blue fog. Stamp mouth, he called it. He'd buy old amateur collections and soak the pages in sugar water until the stamps floated off the paper, then drying them out, licked and mounted them into new albums. He never married. Don't see the point, he said. He'd been intimate with all kinds of people by licking stamps: soldiers writing letters from the trenches, lonely housewives, hotel suicides. It was his way of traveling, of making love to the world. Even after he was gone, the stamp collector said, his licks would still be here.

I Have a Broken, I Have a Broken

It is with sadness we communicate the passing of the zoo-keeper. His neighbors had for some time complained of the lingering odor of wild animals in his apartment, but what troubled the zookeeper and his wife was the vintage chandelier the previous tenant had illegally installed. It dangled from the ceiling with crystal bulbs and twisted candelabra that looked like octopus tentacles. It hung so low that to pass through the room to his favorite arm-chair the zookeeper had to crane his neck at an awkward angle to avoid knocking his head against the chandelier. To make matters worse, the electrical wiring was poor and constantly short circuited, and when the zookeeper tried to fix the wiring he only succeeded in mildly electrocuting himself, much to the dismay of his wife. During these electrical outages, their increasingly embittered relation-ship was only salvaged by torrid sessions of intercourse. After his wife unexpectedly died last year, the zookeeper discovered that every time he walked into the room he became aroused recalling his previous romances on the floor and had to sit in his armchair until he was no longer flustered. The pain of such memories encouraged the zoo-keeper to dispose of both the armchair and the chandelier. Recently, the zookeeper walked through the room and, without thinking, craned his neck as if the chandelier was still there, after which he became aroused and attempted to sit on the absent armchair. Returning from the hos-pital with a fractured coccyx, he walked through the room and, without thinking, craned his neck once more and attempted to sit once again on the absent armchair. It took several days before the neighbors phoned the authorities, assuming the noises coming from the apartment were the sadness of a grieving widower, or another wild animal the zookeeper had rescued, or their minds were playing tricks on them, or in the very least, a ghost. Following a lengthy recovery, the zookeeper celebrated with a game of Mormon basketball. Dead of a heart attack. He was sixty-two.

Come, Come Ye Saints

It is with sadness we communicate the unexpected death of the jury member and, as such, must postpone selection of the prize-winning performance at this year's Marx Jubilee. We ask for patience in this difficult time. Each spring, as everyone knows, fifth grade students all over Calypsee perform reenactments of Karl Marx's little-known visit to Utah in 1875. He'd come at the behest of Brigham Young who hoped to convince the eccentric German that theocratic capitalism was the ideal economic system, but Marx was more interested in seeking a cure at the sanatorium for his pleurisy. He made a stop in Calypsee but no official record of his visit survives. The reenactments have grown in popularity over the years. Competition is fierce. Some students spend all year preparing and have thus awakened the thespian spirit of the town. A jury selects the best performance to send to the International Marx Festival in Trier. Gracious funding for the lucky winner is provided by the Le Moist Toilet Paper Corporation whose factory is the oldest employer in town. As every child who passes through our esteemed public education system knows, when the nine founding polygamist families established Calypsee there was nothing but sand and sagebrush. Pretty soon these pioneers were abridging the lyrics of a favorite hymn to reflect their angst: *Come, come ye Saints/ No toilet paper here/ Not even grass/ to wipe your ass.* Years later, a local chemist engineered a new formula to manufacture toilet paper from sand. It was known as the Gentle Gentile Bath Tissue Company for almost one hundred years until the company was recently purchased in bankruptcy by an international Japanese conglomerate who changed the name because French sounds more sophisticated. These new Le Moist rolls are not moist at all but come in a variety of scents for whatever kind of anus you want: peach, orange, peppermint, licorice, and so on. They have fancy names like *Merlot with Night Sky* and *Lemon Drop Island*. Personally, we prefer the old sandy style whose billboard just outside of town says *Don't Stop Excreting!* which should only be said with gusto to the tune of Journey's "Don't Stop Believin.'" A statue of Marx sitting on the toilet outside the factory was donated by the good citizens of Trier during the 1950s Red Scare with the inscription, LOVE THY NEIGHBOR FOR EVEN COMMUNISTS POOP. Tours are open to the public Monday through Thursday and come with a free roll of toilet paper, some scents excluded.

Of Hominins

It is with sadness we communicate the passing of the Reverend of St. Emmanuel Lutheran on East Elm Street. Not a Mormon, but all things are forgivable, eventually. When the Reverend left Germany at the turn of the century to start his church in our town, a church which he described in his diary would conquer the seven-headed dragon prophesied in the Book of Revelation, nineteen relatives followed. Only his brother stayed behind. No photographs of the brother exist, but his medical records are known to us. His heart weighed 11 grams at birth. The doctor diagnosed arrhythmia and said the child would not live through the night. The boy's mother, who believed science was a conspiracy of fallen angels, sang to the boy while he sucked her breast. It was her voice, she said, that taught his heart how to beat. When his heart weighed 41 grams he was expelled from school for mindlessness. It weighed 72 grams when he saw the meteor shower and stopped believing in God. It weighed 104 grams the morning he spied the neighbor on the balcony reading French poetry in her underwear. It was the foreign words, not her nudity, he later said, that cured his arrhythmia. When his heart weighed 274 grams, he disobeyed his mother and sailed to Antarctica on the Valdivia. He wore a deep-sea diving suit and sank to the ocean floor. Hours later he returned with stories of strange fish and architectural ruins. Nobody believed him. When the war began his heart weighed 295 grams. When it ended it weighed 309 grams. It weighed 294 grams when love disillusioned him for the last time. It weighed 304 grams when he took a position writing radio jingles, a job he worked for the next five decades without a measurable effect on his heart. His heart weighed 318 grams when he was praised by the German Scientific Society for publishing an article advancing the theory that cities of the future would be powered by human bio-fuel. It weighed 337 grams when he began broadcasting radio jingles soliciting human research subjects: *Take it from your rabbi/ it's as easy as toasting rye/ Liquefy! Liquefy!* His heart weighed 347 grams the night he tested his experimental machine. A neighbor collected the puddle of him. It weighed 351 grams. After the second war, the Reverend collected his brother's remains along with a few personal artifacts and brought them to our town. Before his own death, the Reverend converted his home into a small museum honoring his brother. Visitors can see the notebook with scribbled equations, a pipe, a chamber pot. In the parlor is a bell jar on a stool. What remains of the Reverend's brother is a pale, yellow liquid, almost translucent. A few drops are added each month, the museum curator tells us, thanks to the generous donations of the public who believe in the soft light of hominins.

Good Housekeeping

An unmarried woman complained to her landlord she was baking a cake for a friend and left several dirty pots and pans in the sink overnight only to discover them cleaned and returned to their rightful place in the cabinet the following morning. Reports of similar incidents were soon commonplace in the apartment complex. Residents stepped out for a few hours, or even a few minutes, and returned to a clean kitchenette. The lawyer in 3G became irritated when the mystery dish washer habitually ignored him, having left his filthy saucepans in the sink for more than a month. For a while he thought it might be the cosmonaut boy who sometimes slept in the boiler room and only ate lime green Jell-O poured down the oxygen hose by the fistful, a boy who had watched so many old sci-fi movies he believed he was an alien, even wearing what looked like a grimy fishbowl for a space helmet every-where as if trying to keep the dreamsick thoughts that blew up in his brain from infecting everyone else. That's not black pepper, the boy's fingers seemed to say at the pizza parlor, those are the leftover radioactive ants from *Them!* And the clothes in the thrift shops hadn't been donated, the cosmonaut boy's fingers seemed to say, but belonged to people liquified by the *H-Man*. And it wasn't because he couldn't swim that he didn't get baptized, he told the dentist, he just didn't want to be like every other creature with an atom brain in this town. Are you one of those nice aliens here on vacation to take in the sights, the dentist asked, or did you come to brainwash and body-snatch?

In all my years skipping in and out of time, you are the saddest motherclucker I have ever met, the cosmonaut boy's fingers seemed to say. You're too late, kid, the dentist said, the Church got here first. The other apartment residents said the dish washer must be a pervert, but the lawyer wasn't so sure. Sometimes he would stand in the doorway of the latest victim and stare at the neat stack of dishes drying on the rack, thinking it was pretty damn artistic, but also afraid because the kitchen is an intimate place and there's something weirdly familiar about cooking and fucking but he couldn't figure out what. Eventually, the lawyer invited other residents to join him for dinner hoping to sleuth the identity of the dish washing perpetrator. He invited over the unmarried woman, the first victim, and they shared many dinners. Despite having lived near her for years the lawyer never noticed the delicacy of her hands scrubbing dishes. Within a few months they were married but the lawyer was incredibly disappointed to learn the woman was nothing like he had imagined and lacked basic housekeeping skills. His new wife suggested they move somewhere else, a home of their own perhaps, with a yard for a dog and a baby, but the lawyer stubbornly insisted on living in the cramped apartment, always leaving a door ajar or a window cracked in the hopes the mystery dish washer would appear. He awoke the morning of his death—an accident according to some and by nefarious design according to others—to find his wife gone, having left everything behind, including last night's dirty dishes in the sink.

Nobody wore the same moth-eaten cardigan every day. It had fat, colored stripes. He said his father gave it to him. Nobody had three fathers. The first was Konstantin Tsiolkovsky, the Russian hermit who invented rocketry. Li Bai, the eighth century poet of many names and many deaths, was his second father. Nobody's fingers seemed to say, I would have known perfect bliss had I been raised by Ward Cleaver.

Nobody knew his real father.

Nobody used to open the refrigerator and watch the bulb flicker. His mother said it started doing that ever since his father left. Nobody put his hand close to the flashing light for hours. He felt the pulse of it crackling and humming. Like it was talking to him. Sometimes he liked to curl inside the fridge like a contortionist. Nobody knew how he did it.

Our fathers said not to play with him. He wasn't baptized. They said he had so many sins they were leaking out of his body. What do you think those oozing pink patches on his knees and elbows are? our fathers said.

Is sin contagious? we wondered. Don't ask questions, our fathers said.

A True Sugarbeeter

It is with sadness we communicate the janitor at the Westside High School died last Sunday by his own hand. He was an alumnus and not just one of the nicest men in town but an ambassador of good hygiene and a true Sugarbeeter. He was the star linebacker in high school and anybody who was alive thirty years ago will remember the big game against the rival Eastside Spuds. It all came down to the fourth quarter where he rallied the defense for a goal line stand before sacking the opposing quarterback and recovering the fumble, returning it all the way down the field before he was regrettably stopped on the four-yard line and prevented from scoring the game-winning touchdown. They lost in overtime. After the game, grainy photos surfaced of him partying the night before with the cheerleaders of the rival team and their potato mascot, engaging in a bawdy rendition of their Mighty Spudder dance which prompted an inquiry from school officials and local law enforcement about whether the future janitor conspired to intentionally lose the game. He professed his innocence and was eventually cleared of all suspicion but after that things fell apart. The Yam Queen broke up with him. His mother died, some say of shame. He lost a scholarship. He was excommunicated from the Mormons, then later disfellowshipped from the Lutherans. He joined the army but was dishonorably discharged. He joined the local chapter of the KKK believing if he poured gasoline on the dumpster fire that is humanity Jesus would see the smoke signal. He started drinking and was in and out of rehab for years, during which time his estranged son refused to visit him. He'd only recently taken the job as the janitor after a long period of homelessness and finally seemed to be putting his life back together, wearing his old letterman's jacket on game days, and buffing his medals late at night while watching grainy video footage of his athletic glory days. We told him he should settle down, find a wife, have a family. Nah, he smiled as he polished the trophy case in the gym, and quit all this cold turkey? One of the students found him dead on the football field. The funeral was held today in the stadium. Following the eulogy, the pallbearers carried the casket down the length of the field where he was buried in the endzone as the cheerleading squad practiced their routine, chanting, WE'RE SO SWEET WE CAN'T BE BEET! as they danced to the tune of "Just Beat It."

My Shangri-La Beneath the Winter Moon

Utah is a possessed place. At the right time of day, buildings long-since torn down are visible, the smell of flowers in imaginary parks are fragrant, and alleys swallowed up by sinkholes reappear like phantom limbs. Stand on a street corner too long and you can still hear laughs, screams, and sighs from pioneers one hundred years ago, their voices just now catching up with the world. In the desert, things that are not there are just as important as things that are. Mormons love their ghosts. They hoard keepsakes of dead relatives in attics, their basements overflowing with boxes of mildewed photographs wedged between jars of canned peaches. On the weekends they flock to their temples and hold hands. They whisper prayers trying to Frankenstein their souls to dead souls, hoping to make a long chain of paper dolls that rings-around-the-rosy of a cosmic family tree. Everyone here is family. Except *les trois soeurs*. Three sisters orphaned by time. We only see them when it snows. Their dark shadows blooming out of white drifts. They're always laughing, hiding moonspun hair under wool caps and asking what time it is in a rudimentary Franglais, worried they have been alive so long and still don't have a family. Sometimes they stay to play games, leading away other children into their limbo. Yesterday, during the first snowfall, school was canceled like always and all the businesses closed as we wandered through town looking for the three sisters. He's not your daddy, the nightgown lady told the cosmonaut boy. She shut the door in his face. The cosmonaut boy watched her shadow through the mottled glass. He sat on the icy porch steps. A dog barked in the yard. The stars blinked dumbly at him. He watched the neighbors turn off their lights. He knocked on the door again. The nightgown lady's shadow pretended not to be home. He came back later and the dentist was on the porch with the lady who now had a rolling pin. You can see him, the dentist said, he's not a ghost, right? I don't know what kind of stupid you're breathing, Dr. Dip, the nightgown lady said, but do all of us a favor and just choke on it. The cosmonaut boy stood in the alley as if he heard little girls laughing, but it was only shadows. Looks like you're stuck with me, the dentist said. The cosmonaut boy stared at the shadows. He moved closer. People just want to fool you, his fingers seemed to say.

A Worshipful Company of Haberdashers

It is with sadness we communicate the passing of the local
haberdasher, last of his trade, who died in his shop on
Wednesday. Or perhaps it was Tuesday. Nobody knows.
The sign under his shop bearing the livery badge of a lion
with a blue tongue and claws had fallen into the gutter
and inside they found the haberdasher hanging from a silk
noose. He'd taken over the trade from his father, whose
father was also a haberdasher, as were his father's father's
fathers, all the way back to when it was known as the
Fraternity of the Mystery of Haberdashers. Now there
was no more mystery, he used to say. People wanted less
scraps. They didn't even want hats anymore. It used to be
a man or woman wouldn't be caught dead in the street
without a hat, the haberdasher lamented to his caged bird,
a gift from his deceased son, but now the only people
who bought them were homosexuals or cancer patients.
The kids said he was one of those old timey mad hatters
sick from mercury poisoning, and others said he suffered
from rapturitis, the kind of sick you can't cure, but the
haberdasher said nobody goes mad because we're all mad
from the start. It was quite a sight, the haberdasher's shop.
Great bolts of fabric floor to ceiling and cubbies of buttons,
zippers, ribbons, and string. The fabric was once spun in
the nearby textile factory—since converted into a prophylactic distribution center—but now it comes from
another desert halfway across the world. Someplace far
away, almost unimaginable. Our haberdasher was always
walking around town picking up bits of thread and other

knickknacks tossed into the landfill. Junk, people said. Treasures, the haberdasher said. For him, these pieces of string too small to use were a kind of rapture. Because it's not easy living in the desert. The land is spread out like a parched tongue. It's a deep, yawning place, full of nothing except maybe the promise of salvation. There's never any rain because the land has already been baptized in blood. Everything is still being stitched together. Streets connecting to streets, cities to cities, and now all these satellites with their invisible signals nobody can see until they come falling out of orbit, leaving burning trails across the sky like marionette strings. The American West is a Frankenstein and Calypsee is just one limb hanging by a thread. You can string just about anything together, the haberdasher used to say, but at any moment it can come unraveled without rhyme or reason. That's why it's nice to have so much sun in the sky. It's made of string too, the haberdasher told the caged bird. A hot boiling knot of vibrating plasma strings. Eight billion years from now the knot will unravel. Before his son died, the haberdasher used to tell customers about the broken band of sunlight his boy had found in the landfill. How he nursed it back to health and claimed he swung from it like a rope when nobody was looking. How he lost it one day when it slipped through the hole in his pocket. The haberdasher hadn't believed his boy and laughed with customers at his boy's wild imagination. But recently we noticed the haberdasher leaning out the window with his dumb face fixed on the sky, as if imagining himself like a tightrope walker at the circus wobbling on a thin thread of sunlight higher and higher.

Scan This Wasted Land

It is with sadness we communicate the passing of the sur-
veyor who went down into the landfill last week and never
returned. It goes by many names. The Pit, the Hollow, the
Onion. God's Junkyard. Those who find the Sphincter
indecent prefer to call it the Sphinx. We have it on good
authority you can almost see it from outer space. It dates
back to the first hours of our town. When the nine polyg-
amous families who settled the area decided *this is the place,*
their first order of business was to pray and thank God
their travels had come to an end. After a loud *Amen,* they
dug a hole for shitting. The following Sunday, that ini-
tial outhouse became the consecrated foundation pit for
the temple they one day hoped to build in the city center.
In the century since, the pit has widened and deepened
as promises of the temple have come and gone. Shovels
for the optimists are available year-round and openings
in the chain-link fence are marked with yellow ribbons.
Nobody is quite sure how deep it goes. At the turn of the
century the local bishop and amateur astronomer declared
an asteroid would shortly hit the planet and, in a panic,
citizens converted the landfill into something of an ark.
They brought mirrors, gramophones, perfume bottles, golf
clubs, shotguns, hymnals, and prophylactics. Later, it filled
with batteries, can openers, refrigerators, narwhal tusks,
plastic sacrament cups, ham radios, dehydrated potato
pearls, dildos, teddy bears, fiddles, corn flakes, church pews,
and toothpaste. The cosmonaut boy is always rummaging
down there, and since repairing a salvaged boom box he

crawls through the chapel window on Sunday nights and dances to Michael Jackson's *Thriller*. He sleeps in alleys and dumpsters and treehouses. The sheep ranchers often find him in their pens. They say he has a way with them, like they know each other's thoughts, which is why the kids at school say he's a sheepfucker. But all he really does is arouse a few of the rams each morning then bottles that lotion to sell to the church ladies promising it will get rid of their wrinkles. These sisters give it to their husbands who wear these overnight beauty masks religiously. Everything in the landfill is a relic of belief. A hairbrush that smells awful and suddenly everyone says Bigfoot lives down there. Once, a half-burnt doll had half the town convinced those who don't go to heaven will have their genitals erased like Ken and Barbie dolls. The most common thing thrown down there is Mormon underwear. Once some of the baseball boys convinced the cosmonaut boy to put on a discarded pair of those silky alien pajamas and then lit them on fire. The boy darted through the streets like a squirrel until the septic man hosed him down with a day's worth of deliveries from his truck. He walked a little funny after that, but nobody noticed a burn on him. Nobody knew if it was the garments or freakshow luck that saved him, but most true-believing Mormons know their underwear's real magic is getting rid of spaghetti stains on the carpet.

Try to Find the Way I Feel

It is with sadness we communicate the passing of the octogenarian cardiologist at the so-called Frogeye Festival, an annual gathering of culinary aficionados who come far and wide each year to celebrate Calypsee as the birthplace of frogeye salad. The dessert—which calls for acini de pepe boiled al dente and mixed with stovetop custard before gently folding in pineapple chunks, mandarin oranges, and marshmallows garnished with shaved coconuts and an ostentatious arrangement of maraschino cherries—was invented by Danes who left Scandinavia because they knew one day the government would mandate socialized medicine and perform studies proving they were the happiest country in the world, but they wanted the freedom to be miserable so they crossed the American frontier and ended up in Utah with no beer, six wives, and a strange dessert that somehow was also a salad. After sampling the desserts and casting his vote, the dentist, the one the kids call Dr. Dip, wandered the mansion listening to lawyers and doctors talk about the bond market and President Reagan, our patron saint, trying to save the country from the communists. When he mentioned he was taking care of the cosmonaut boy, the Relief Society ladies in puffy blazers asked, Good heavens, they awarded you custody of the retarded kid? Somebody has to do what nobody else will, the dentist said. He's one of those space children, the church ladies said. He's a cuckoo clock who can't tell time, the dentist said. What does that mean? they asked. The dentist shrugged. During the white elephant exchange, the dentist's gift was the first to be opened: an anal plug with bright letters on the package that said RED CHIEF. The dentist had purchased it from the Kinkalypse, a so-called Christian sex shop downtown. The octogenarians took turns passing it around, guessing what it might be, giggling when it lit up and wondering if it was a child's night-light, or perhaps a Christmas ornament, or maybe one of those lamps that if you rub it the genie comes out, when the cardiologist suddenly realized what he was holding and collapsed unconscious. While the dentist performed CPR, the other octogenarians told stories about the bow-tied cardiologist, like how before sedating patients he whispered in their ears *I'm going to fuck you up*, or that time he ate wild mushrooms and hallucinated the mailbox was trying to eat him, and while the police investigated whether his passing was a homicide or merely death by misadventure, the dentist went home and looked out the window hoping for the cosmonaut boy to come snooping around the porch. He ate a warm, soggy bowl of frogeye salad. He spun the Red Chief on the table, wondering why some things happen to some people but not to others, why some are actors on the stage and others the crew manipulating the lights, but what he couldn't figure out was why most of us are the audience sitting in the dark, and he felt on the cusp of some great feeling—of almost being a character worthy of an anecdote, kind of like frogeye salad which is almost edible.

And Otherwise Infirmed

Yesterday, an unidentified man leapt from the highway overpass into oncoming traffic. A produce truck swerved to avoid the falling man and then flipped, spilling hundreds of cantaloupes onto the highway. The truck driver and his son were ejected from the vehicle during the collision. While their bodies have since been recovered, both father and son were decapitated, their heads catapulted onto the highway and lost among the scattered fruit. Volunteers continue to comb the surrounding brush, prying back tall grasses in search of the wayward remains. Despite the horrible accident, the annual fruit festival continued as planned. A new cantaloupe queen was crowned. The boys outside her window said she stayed up all night in her orange dress with a white sash practicing her wave, imagining how she would smile at the crowd from the parade float as she bit into cantaloupe slices.

Out of Mercy

The Fotomat kiosk was in the strip mall parking lot. The photo clerk watched the dropout skateboarders. He studied the faces of children on milk cartons. Occasionally, strangers tapped on the window with a roll of film. Two hours, the photo clerk said without looking up. He used to own his own photo studio. He had a darkroom with all the fancy jars, thermometers, developers, stabilizers, blixers. He could still see the shop through the kiosk window next to the supermarket, the windows boarded up and a yellowed FOR LEASE sign. Before he would stand for hours developing photos, enchanted by the process. Now he put the film into a machine and it spit out perfectly clear photos. Now he watched Reagan on the portable television threaten to shoot the Russians with laser beams from outer space It's all machines now, he told the lizards bathing in the shadows, everything translated into a zero or a one. Little Boy: 1. Tsar Bomba: 0. Chernobyl: 1. Three Mile Island: 0. Fischer: 1. Spassky: 0. He missed his studio. He missed mixing the chemicals. He missed overexposures, light leaks, and backscatter. He missed the shadows, blurs, smears, and chemical burns. He missed waiting, the image slowly coming into focus. He missed the mistakes and the accidental mysteries, because every time you looked at an old photo you saw a different story, the photo clerk said. Not like photos now where everything is crisp, clean, sterile, fixed. He liked a look of ruin. Sometimes he rescued old grainy photos from thrift shops so that they didn't have to feel so lonely. Sometimes he walked along the highway

at night photographing roadkill. If he was lucky, he found
a mutilated sheep drained of all its blood. No tracks or
footprints nearby. Ears, eyes, udders, and tongues deli-
cately posed on the asphalt. UFOs, he told the cosmonaut
boy who often stopped by the Fotomat kiosk. The photo
clerk developed these photos in the apartment bathtub
now, arranging the botched images into a mural on his
apartment wall, including the one he took of the war veteran's mad dog that escaped the apartment last night and
mauled a young girl playing with sidewalk chalk. After
the incident, the girl's distraught father, a gastroenterologist, knocked on the war veteran's door and proceeded to
bludgeon the animal with a marble paperweight shaped
like a caduceus he received as a graduation gift. The girl,
disfigured for life, is expected to recover. When asked why
he put down the poor creature, the gastroenterologist said,
Out of mercy.

An Artful Pose

It is with sadness we communicate the passing of a woman who went to Hollywood seeking fame and returned to Calypsee after many years. Nothing was how she remembered it. It seemed both larger and smaller to her than before, both quaint and ugly, deserted and overpopulated, and everything foreign—from the parks and buildings to the smell of scones in the bakery. The woman wandered for hours looking for the fountain where she spent so many Sundays feeding pigeons after church, but never found it. The only recognizable building was St. Garfield's Art Academy where she was a once promising student convinced she was destined for international fame as a mime. She was only fourteen the afternoon a school bus with a dozen children caught fire after it tumbled down the ravine. In her ecstasy, she had not summoned the fire department, mistaking the burning bus for part of the upcoming performance exams. The theatre professors were horrified when they found her expertly miming the inferno to a crowd of onlookers. Witnesses who saw the Hollywood woman moments before she was run over by the trolley said she was dancing in the rain and they believed she was insane. They said they didn't hear any music.

I Will Return Again

It is with sadness we communicate the passing of the repo man, a real adrenaline junkie. First dirt bikes, then rock climbing and pinfinger games. He played Russian roulette on the weekends. He drank nine cups of coffee a day. For a while he was part of an optimism cult practicing random acts of kindness which he said was the craziest high but also exhausting. Inspired by the Emilio Estevez movie, he started a repo business and stayed up late watching QVC on the cable convertor box he'd repossessed. His apartment was full of shower radios, bunion pads, and chest expanders. He never wore a shirt, showing off his chest hair that grew in thick, peculiar designs like crop circles. Everyone said he shaved it like that himself, but the cosmonaut boy told him he was being abducted by aliens at night who wiped his memory clean. Did they get you too? the repo man asked, and the cosmonaut boy said the aliens had abducted him so many times, taking him apart and putting him back together so often, like a Humpty Dumpty, that whenever he walked through doors he time traveled. A closet or a fridge or even crawling through a window—he'd come out the other side the same place and the same life, just another time, like a rock skipped over a lake, as if time is a cosmonaut, his fingers seemed to say. The repo man believed his crop circle chest hair was more likely a government experiment, like when he was a baby and had fine lips and a nicely circumcised penis, but after the Air Force doctors ran their tests he came back hare-lipped and uncircumcised. But you know what really keeps me up at night? It wasn't Chernobyl or salamander letters, but Fibonacci numbers. Math is such a strange drug, he told the widow who stabbed him in the throat with an ice pick last night, because everything in nature is a spiral if you zoom in close enough. He let her touch his weird chest hair and said it didn't seem possible that these curls were the same spiral as a snail's shell which was mathematically no different from the spiral of the Milky Way. Even the swirl of the sourdough crust baked in a golden ratio. It was the recipe his great-great-great-grandmother carried across the plains with other pioneer Mormons. The secret, the repo man told the widow as he held the jar of fermented dough to her nose, is in the yeast that's one hundred and thirty-nine years old.

Nobody told us we bordered the 37th parallel. The UFO superhighway. Home to mutilated sheep, salt flats, Paiute holy grounds, nuclear silos, creosote, skinwalkers, spinning compass needles, the Midnight Massacre, singing sand dunes, abductions, jellyfish sprites, marlstone valleys, lizard people, patriots, petroglyphs, and a murmur at night coming out of the dust that causes dizziness and insomnia and polygamist dreams.

Nobody climbed up the lampposts and telephone poles and satellite dish antennas and moved his fingers at the sky, as if signaling to something he wanted to be abducted.

Nobody walked everywhere with a parabolic microphone recording desert sounds. He said it doubled as an alien death-ray. When we listened, all we heard was static.

Nobody's favorite thing in the world was orchids. He stole them from the florist but was always looking for them in the wild. Fairy slippers, his fingers seemed to call them, because the petals were arched like Cinderella's foot. His fingers seemed to tell us they grew in shady canyon bogs where rattlesnakes hibernate and bees wander until tricked into the spotted orchid pouch hoping for nectar but finding none. Pollination by deception, Nobody's fingers seemed to say. Whenever the baseball boys ran after him, the petals fell out of Nobody's pockets like purple raindrops. He twisted them together into all kinds of strange shapes, like a mandala, or a star, or a baseball, and left them in mailboxes and on bus stops and tree stumps. Nobody understood why he did it, only that sometimes you do things for the pleasure of it.

Nobody knew if he really was a deaf mute. Sometimes we thought we heard something inside that helmet. Nobody screaming for us to listen, but we just didn't hear. Other times it was deathly quiet, and nobody said anything.

Nobody talked with his hands, the fingers like thin white dreams, too quick for anyone in town to understand, so nobody bothered. Other times he kept his hands in his pockets, or hidden behind his back, almost as if he was ashamed or perhaps the master of some great secret nobody could figure out. He picked cherries. He petted stray dogs. He plunged the hands into an icy pond as if trying to get the fingers to stop speaking.

Nobody slouched against a brick wall downtown, hands in his pockets, the helmet swaying to some tune nobody else could hear, as if behind that soap scummed helmet he was watching everyone else's hands, waiting for someone to talk back.

Ketchup, Not Catsup

It is with sadness we communicate the passing of the Avon lady, an avid collector of all things ketchup. She started young, shoplifting sachets from the local diner, until eventually the garage was full of empty bottles. In the attic she kept boxes of ketchup kitsch: earrings, bracelets, pins, stickers, key chains, crocheted tomatoes, lip balm, even ketchup-flavored prophylactics. People said she bathed in ketchup and that's why her skin was so soft and unwrinkled. Her husband, a short order cook at the diner, said she never ate ketchup, not even with fries. She didn't like the taste of it, he said. They'd been divorced for years but still lived together, putting aside their lingering, irreconcilable differences, like how the Avon lady always spelled it *catsup* on the grocery list. It's ketchup, not catsup, he always argued, confessing he was willing to forgive most flaws but could not in good conscience respect a woman with poor grammar, then off to the store to make amends by purchasing her a bouquet of flowers. They're artificial, the Avon lady complained yesterday when he returned. The cook told her real flowers die but these would brighten the room through the winter, but she would not be consoled. You think too much to be sane, he told her. Men just don't understand, the Avon lady said, men never think what a woman wants.

Oh, Baby, I Been Blind

The waitress at the diner ate slices of cherry pie and drank cola on every shift hoping to get a cavity. She was in love with the dentist and once a month went to get her teeth cleaned. One night, after the end of her shift, she asked if the dentist would give her a ride home and sat in his little red truck with broken seatbelts while he mumbled along to a Led Zeppelin song. She pretended to be interested when he told her about each different tooth and what its name was and how it had a different job and how he loved their weird shapes and the democracy of how they grind everything down to mush. I love teeth because they're optimistic fatalists, the dentist said. She couldn't tell if he was joking or being serious, and she felt like she was supposed to say something too, something smart or funny, so she told him she had been born with holes in her heart and the doctor said it could affect her weight, so her parents worried she might float away and tied a string around her foot to the bedpost. She grew up without hardly ever leaving the room, her mother worried she'd never get to say I have a broken heart, just *I have a broken, I have a broken,* until one night the waitress snuck out the window to go dancing. Her parents, who gambled away all their money at the Indian casino trying to pay for the heart surgery, drank rat poison believing she floated away. What about your heart? the dentist asked. The waitress shrugged. Sometimes the holes close on their own and sometimes the hole never heals and swallows the heart. They stopped at an antique shop where the dentist wandered around touching things: a lamp, a marionette, tools in a toolbox, and a movie camera from the 1920s. The waitress went back later and bought everything the dentist touched. She lay in bed thinking about his weird bird's nest of hair and his voice like grilled cheese burnt in a skillet. For months, she tried to think of a clever way to confess her love, like writing on his receipt, *Do you want to box me up and take me home?* But instead she just wrote, *I think I love you.* The dentist—who had tried telling her he was no good and that she'd be better off with someone young and foolish—left without paying and never came back. After, the waitress stood in the bathroom with the antique hammer and tapped it against her teeth. A woman washing her hands at the sink pressed the hammer claw against the waitress's neck and told her she'd bleed better from there. They are now lovers raising chickens in a farmhouse outside of town.

Nobody liked to walk far out into the desert. Past the sandstone canyons where the men laid off from the uranium mines got drunk, past the alfalfa farms, and into the salt flats. That's where he found the rooster head. The face was swollen and its prickly red comb had turned dull yellow, its eyes two pale marbles with black slits like a weird door left ajar. Nobody said he found it in a cave, but we were pretty sure he'd stolen it from the farmer at the State Fair who charged a quarter to see his headless chicken walk around the stage. No strings! the farmer said, everyone believing it was a bona fide miracle. Nobody said the rooster head was as old as The Beast from 20,000 Fathoms. *He pickled it in a jar of formaldehyde. We watched it float.*

Nobody called it Syzygy. He carried it with him everywhere.

Nobody could hear what it said. It was Syzygy who told Nobody where to find the accordion in the landfill. It was Syzygy who helped him hide from the Mormon bishop always trying to baptize him. It was Syzygy who showed him how to map the constellations to find his way back home. It was Syzygy who told him where to find the NASA satellites that didn't burn up in the atmosphere and crashed on their return from orbit. It was Syzygy who helped him build the ham radio.

It was Syzygy who told him which sci-fi movies to watch.

Nobody loved sci-fi movies. Sometimes he pantomimed them on the playground. He was the mad scientist breeding carnivorous plants and resurrecting the dead in The Woman Eater. *He*

spent hours practicing his telepathy like the Cat Women of the
Moon. *He jumped through the school window after watching*
4D-Man. *His favorite was* Space Master X-7 *about a cosmic
fungus colonizing earth. See? his fingers seemed to say, showing
us the dark scales on his elbows like tree bark, like he was some
weird* Pinocchio—*I'm an alien.*

*Nobody enjoyed living in mismatched alphabets. Our words,
his fingers. It was like he wanted to be misunderstood. They
hated him not because he went crazy to survive this place, but
because he wanted us to go crazy with him.*

Unspeakable Pleasures

It is with sadness we communicate the passing of the hotel concierge who, three hours before he supposedly fell down an empty elevator shaft, was busy arranging the breakfast buffet. The cereals in their dispenser bins. The fruits on their platters. The coffee maker hissing. The eggs and bacon and hashbrowns steaming in their pans. He took extra care with the oatmeal packets. He arranged rows for each flavor: maple and brown sugar, apples and cinnamon, peaches and cream, rum raisin. Packaged oatmeal, the concierge was convinced, was a staple of hotel breakfast buffets not because of its ease of preparation but due to a centuries-old hospitality practice where oatmeal is reserved for those sad married couples with at least three children who have not yet mastered the Transient Coital Quickie. Those who had mastered the TCQ rewarded themselves with a carnivore diet. The rest ate oatmeal. The concierge scribbled on a napkin the probabilistic equation for TCQ where Q represents the quickie quotient:

$$Q = \frac{\overline{(R \times G \times L)}}{(M \times \lambda)}$$

R represents the erotic ambiance, G is the arousal factor of the geographic location, L is the lighting, M is the length of marriage, and lambda is Fibonacci's Constant (d x P x v, or desperation times position times velocity), named after the bachelor Italian mathematician. An amateur sociologist, the concierge rated his hotel adequate on erotic ambiance, having an appealing bed size, pleasant décor, no noticeable odors, and a pool. Geography fair. Lighting questionable. He lived for the breakfast service. He stood in the lobby and studied the faces of male travelers, theorizing who would eat oatmeal and who would not. The sunburnt wiry man with two-day stubble. The pudgy bespectacled gentleman dressed for a day of golf. With each man he shared a brief glimpse, smiled, then looked away.

Not a Word I Heard Could I Relate

The social worker, who until recently we believed was a pathologically charitable woman with a smile that masked a good deal of pain from caring for the foster children of Calypsee, was found hanged yesterday. She spent the morning of her death supervising the dentist, inspecting the property and making note of the train track scars on the cosmonaut boy's arms and feet, trying to make sense of the trebuchet schematics he showed her and the rapid fluttering of his fingers. He doesn't say much, the dentist told her, demonstrating how he rubbed lotion on the boy's scaly red elbows and knees and saying he was the only one who'd been kind to the boy, this little dumbsaint he called him after reading it in a book, even though the boy's fingers seemed to say, This isn't kind. The social worker asked if the boy was getting the help he needed, and the cosmonaut boy's fingers seemed to say, Nobody knows what the cluck you're talking about. The dentist said they planned on going to church more often as the social worker filled out a report of the latest incident, the cosmonaut boy correcting her that, yes, he had mooned a passing motorist on the highway and, naturally, his warm butt pressed against the cold windshield cracked the glass and, yes, it caused the dentist to fishtail into a ditch and, pulling down his pants to show her the wound, resulted in thirteen stitches for him, but he'd done it because he worried the woman driving next to them might have an alien parasite attached to her spine, a tingler, so he dropped his pants because a scream at the right time might save her life. He paced the room with his accordion, playing the same notes over and over like the eerie soundtrack from *The Mesa of Lost Women*. The dentist said, Why don't you play this lady some Led Zeppelin, or at least something that doesn't sound so terrible? I wrote this song, the cosmonaut boy's fingers seemed to say, I call it *No Jesus Summer*. He was naked except for a well-positioned sock over his scabbed little alien prick. He thinks he's playing, the dentist smiled at the social worker. The cosmonaut boy's fingers seemed to say that he liked the wrong notes, that he too was just a little out of tune and he didn't like people without a sense of bewilderness. The dentist, who wasn't sure if the conversation was funny or sad, excused himself to the bathroom where he had a whippit, feeling himself shrinking smaller and smaller as if he were a fly yet somehow heavy as an elephant. Two more whippits and it took every effort to keep his face from floating away. His life flashed before his eyes and he wasn't even in it. The social worker knocked on the bathroom door. The cosmonaut boy played the accordion louder. The dentist locked the door and hid in the tub. You're naked, the social worker said, prying back the shower curtain. But not nude, the dentist said. The more the social worker tried to speak over the cosmonaut boy's music the louder he played. Eventually, she gave up.

Nobody started huffing paint thinner in third grade art class. When his mom was sick, he stole her meds: hydros, benzos, laudanum, Thorazine. His favorite was the cat tranquilizer he stole from the veterinarian's office. Ketamine. Special K. Like his mother used to say. Don't mind this town. You're special, 'k? By the time he dropped out of school he had come to think of life as a plane crash and drugs were the parachute.

He ran away from the foster home. He slept in a refrigerator in the landfill.

Nobody believed he time traveled. He said it was unpredictable. Walking onto the bus or crawling through a window. It just happened. He'd lost track of time wandering across hours and in and out of years under this ocean of stars.

They gave him electroshock therapy twice a week at the State Hospital.

The bishop tried to convince him it was all in his head. He laid his hands on Nobody's fishbowl helmet and prayed for him to be baptized. Don't you want to be one of us? Of all the tribes, in all the deserts, in all the worlds, you found the one true church. Leave the junk alone already. Wouldn't you rather be addicted to the Lord?

For Sale, Cancer, Gently Used

The woman purchased the cancer at the school bake sale last spring. They told her it was a Swedish cardamom bun, all knotted and whorled and not quite baked right, but the woman knew it was a cancer. Once home, she left it on the counter while she cleaned the house. Later, she found it near the window as if contemplating suicide. It oozed clear jelly. The cancer smelled suspicious, so she gave it a bath and rubbed off the scabbed crusts. She patted it dry, ignoring the soured odor. Unbuttoning her blouse, she held it to her breast. Her nipple dangled there like a fishing lure, but the cancer wouldn't take the bait. They read books, played hopscotch, and built a bird house. The birds were more interested in the cancer than the seeds and pecked furiously until it was riddled with holes. When her husband came home, the woman was wrapping the cancer in bacon and smothering it in ketchup. It's a new recipe, she smiled. She watched through the oven window as it bubbled blood and fat and hardened into a knot. She poured herself a glass of wine in the laundry room where her husband couldn't hear her, then drank the glass she didn't have a few hours ago, and then another for a few hours from now. She pretended to eat, resenting it when her husband took a second portion, something he never did with anything else she cooked. Later, she imagined it was the cancer and not her husband's tongue burrowing inside her. The next morning the cancer was swollen, almost twice as big as the night before. It pulsed on the windowsill near the empty bassinet. During Sunday school, the cosmonaut boy looked at the woman with the swaddled cancer tucked in her arm and his fingers seemed to tell her his mother once had a cancer in her breast that burned and itched and came in pulses, like an alien radio signal calling her home. In some other life I could have been a mother to you, the woman told the cosmonaut boy, but I got my own crazy to deal with. She often gave him a glass of lemonade when he wandered by the house and once took him to the movie theatre to watch *The Lady and the Monster*. After church, the woman went to the playground on Pill Hill and buried the cancer in the sandbox. She went back every day until one afternoon she saw a boy tossing the cancer high in the air, like two friends playing catch. The woman's husband tells friends and neighbors his wife is visiting her sister in Pocatello, but we saw her wake up early one morning and walk into the desert. Nobody could save her. The school bake sale finishes tomorrow. All goods half off.

The Story Was Quite Clear

It is with sadness we communicate the passing of the street sweeper, a curious man who came home from the war with a scar above his ear shaped like a pretzel. There was talk he had one of those Japanese microchips in his brain, and soon everyone would have one, the old timers said, but the city hired him anyway as a street sweeper. He saved the newspaper from the gutters and, drying them out on clotheslines, folded them into paper hats which he wore religiously, saying they helped block out the nightmares in which he was still in the war collecting bodies greased in napalm from the DMZ. Sometimes the bodies kept talking even though they had no faces, and sometimes instead of blood and viscera the corpses leaked lemon drops and licorice wheel like the ones his father made in the confectionary shop, and if anyone asked what happened during the war he'd say it's all bewilderness out there and the body is just a strange box of candy then kept sweeping. On the weekends he set up a kiosk at the mall recruiting for the Army. The cosmonaut boy, fresh off a bump of Special K, listened as the street sweeper told stories of what was happening in Grenada and Beirut. Rolling out a constellation map, he showed the crowd of boys the galaxy clusters already being partitioned between Russia and the USA. World War Three will be fought in outer space. Nobody will hear the screams, he said. Everyone signed the dotted line.

Alone, Together

Two hours before the house went up in flames, the barber opened his bedroom curtains. He listened for radon gas bubbling up through the soil. The bird in the tree seemed to call his name. Smoking a cigarette, he showed his wife, a childless PTA president, the scars on his fingers. The sky was the color of a radioactive oyster bed. Naked, the barber and his wife carefully searched the newspaper obituaries. When they made love, it was not as themselves. They pretended to be someone else, calling each other by the names of those recently deceased.

Unhinged

It is with sadness we communicate the passing of the meter maid, a pudgy man who popped fen-phen like tic-tacs but kept getting fat. He weighed himself many times a day, turning side to side at every mirror or window while sucking in his gut, a habit that aggravated his asthma but provided a brief illusion of thinness. He never missed a day of work. He never ignored an expired meter. He never told anyone about seeing the dentist near the trailer park stomping out the embers of the half-burnt catapult. Mormons did this, the dentist said. Mothercluckers, the cosmonaut boy's fingers seemed to say, slumping in the rubble. You're the sorriest looking alien I've ever seen, the dentist said. You're not very helpful, the cosmonaut boy's fingers seemed to say. The truth is, the dentist said, the Mormons burn down your little catapult then go to church on Sundays and talk of angels and forgiveness, but not one of them can tell you what color a calypso orchid is, not one of them has smelled heaven in the midst of hell. After a long day of issuing parking tickets, the meter maid liked to take off his shoes and smell his socks. His wife said it was disgusting, but he enjoyed the smell of honest work. He hand-washed the socks in the sink, hanging them out to dry on the clothesline. He was afraid of electric dryers. As a boy, he and his friend once took turns climbing inside one abandoned in a roadside ditch. His friend got stuck inside and the meter maid wandered off to get help but ended up at the double feature of *Terror from the Year 5000* and *Attack of the Crab Monsters*. Ever since it nauseated him to be around laundry equipment, thinking about his friend screaming into the dark, because even as a child the meter maid believed to die in this life was to wake up in your next one, each death opening up like Russian dolls stacked inside each other, going deeper and deeper but never arriving at the center of yourself. Yesterday, the meter maid went to hang his socks on the clothesline and found his wife of thirty-four years chopping down a tree with an axe she'd borrowed from the neighbor. She had doused it in lighter fluid, but it wouldn't catch. She hacked at the stump and roots until it looked like a retarded heart. Blight is spreading, he said. You're right, she said, and swung the axe.

A Ditmarsh Tale

Services for the baseball boys killed by the drunk driver will be held tomorrow. Mourners are reminded to use the overflow parking available at the creamery on Orange Street. The trio of boys, high school dropouts part of a heavy metal garage band, are survived by their friend, an avid skateboarder who miraculously evaded the same fate. Passersby saw him yesterday at the intersection where the accident happened constructing a small memorial shrine out of cigarettes. He'd been friends with the dead boys for years, but only recently joined the band after the previous bassist broke his arm falling off a roof. He wrote all the lyrics. He told people at church if they sang the songs backwards it would summon Satan, even though he knew it wasn't true. He was only pretending to like heavy metal. He still wore He-Man underwear and collected baseball cards. Most nights he locked his bedroom door and practiced dancing in front of the mirror, dreaming of becoming the next Donny Osmond. As he stared at the cigarette shrine surrounded by candles and photos of the dead boys, he saw a large octopus crawl out of a nearby manhole. It was followed by four hatchlings. The little mollusk family crossed the dusty street one by one. The mother octopus, looking pale and flimsy with one of her arms half-chewed off, paused in the middle of the street. She eyed the skateboarder. Her skin pulsed in slow, sleepy pulses. Then she vanished around the corner, like she knew where she was going.

Nightbrights

It is with sadness we communicate the passing of the old lamplighter who died following an accident. He'd been out of work ever since electricity came to town half a century ago. He said we'd regret all these wires carrying their alien effluvium. He said we'd miss the old light. At the funeral potluck inside the church, the cosmonaut boy couldn't tell if the Jell-O was in fact the parasitic slime from *The Creeping Unknown*, so he went table to table trying to wash it out of old ladies' mouths with a fire extinguisher. The dentist told the boy he was tired of all this pretending, saying there was no mothership in outer space coming to take him home, and the cosmonaut boy's fingers seemed to call him a real motherclucker. They went to the movies. This is the best of all possible churches, the cosmonaut boy's fingers seemed to say as the lights dimmed. We should go back to church, the dentist said. God is an alien and movies are his prophecies, the cosmonaut boy's fingers seemed to say. This is ridiculous, the dentist said halfway through *Forbidden Planet*, how do you watch this nonsense? Some nights, the cosmonaut boy's fingers seemed to say, I watch the triple feature and think God is hiding in the movie trying to show me the way home. After seeing the tiger vaporized the dentist whispered, This isn't fucking Shakespeare, let's go have a bump. I can't imagine how lonely people felt before the movies, the cosmonaut boy's fingers seemed to say. The dentist said he couldn't take a bump by himself anymore because once you share a needle with someone it's like your tongues are twisted around the same prayer. Sometimes I feel like God is everywhere making a list of all the shit I do wrong, the dentist said. The cosmonaut boy's fingers seemed to say, Haven't you heard anything I said? Walking home, the dentist said, You know you're not really an alien, right? You're just a fucked-up kid like the rest of us. The cosmonaut boy drew a picture of a penis on a napkin. The dentist said, What are you telling me? You're a fag? The cosmonaut boy jabbed the dentist in the chest with his finger as if to say, You're a dick. You know the Mormons think I'm a loser, the dentist said. They used to love me but now they say I'm bitter and cruel and hopeless like salt that lost its savor. The cosmonaut boy scratched the pink scaly patches on his elbows until they bled. We're all in this soup together, the dentist said, but here I am swimming. We're all being boiled alive, but why am I the only one doing cannonballs? Nobody cares, the cosmonaut boy's fingers seemed to say, that I'm nobody. He shut the bedroom door behind him. When the dentist opened it, the lights were off and the boy was gone. They buried the lamplighter with his hands in his pockets. They were charred and disfigured after he grabbed the dangling power line after the storm, but somehow strangely aglow with a dull, spent light. For some time, we'd seen him walking back and forth beneath the electric lampposts all night, hypnotized by their soft neon calligraphy. Things change, the lamplighter always said, except light. In the end it eats you. That's what light does.

Thinking of You Without Seeing You

The travel agent went door-to-door with his bouquets of fairy slipper orchids. I grow them in my garden, he told the housewives who invited him inside for lemonade and complimented him on his high-waisted pink pastel pants and alligator skin boots. The housewives thumbed brochures with places they'd never heard of: Turku, Bali, Tangier. The travel agent promised them an escape from this dreary little desert. Six months, three months, two weeks. You're selling fantasies, the housewives said. Time is a fantasy, the travel agent laughed. He stopped briefly at the dentist's house where the cosmonaut boy was on the porch listening to the dentist talk about his father, a rancher, but more of a hemorrhoid with legs, a man who refused to own a car and preferred to ride a stallion to church every Sunday where he corrected the bishop and said after God made woman he repented and created the horse. From sunrise to sunset, he'd ride them and brush them and smile for them and whisper secrets in their ears but wouldn't so much as give the dentist a handshake. The cosmonaut boy's fingers seemed to say, You're going to leave me too, aren't you? The dentist said as a boy he dreamed of winning the Triple Crown, but first his spine twisted so he had to live three years in a brace, and then he grew too big and too tall too fast, his father saying God put too much holiness in his spirit, and he was too clumsy for the rodeo, so he stayed on the ranch, sometimes taming the wild horses but mostly gelding stallions. Your kid doesn't look like you, the travel agent said. I hope not, the dentist said, I'm much uglier. The cosmonaut boy snatched the fairy slipper pinned to the travel agent's lapel. He held the wilted petals against the space helmet. Can you even smell? the dentist asked. You gentlemen interested in a time share? the travel agent asked. I'm retarded, the cosmonaut boy's fingers seemed to say, through time. What's he saying? the travel agent asked. He's retarded, the dentist said, but don't let that fool you. He's the sharpest knife in the drawer. You're sick, you know that? the travel agent said as he headed to the house next door. But the dentist said what was really sick was after his father died, he shot the old man's horses and watched the vultures pick their bones clean. The cosmonaut boy pointed at the sky. Don't listen to those stars, the dentist said after a whippit, they're not your pickle. I bet I could hit a Nolan Ryan fastball, the cosmonaut boy's fingers seemed to say. Like you're just here, just dust, the dentist said, like fucking Sisyphus. Dodger fans are the syphilis of the sports world, the cosmonaut boy's fingers seemed to say. If you buy a time share you get a bouquet, the travel agent told the mechanic through the screen door. He tapped his foot on the welcome mat. Believing this was a secret gay signal, the mechanic with a Deseret Nation beehive tattoo on his arm chased the travel agent around the neighborhood with a machete. The new travel agent—with his brochures about Nauvoo, Pocatello, and Colonia Juárez—is much more successful. He wears dull suits with no flowers on his lapel. Nobody visits his office. He doesn't wave, doesn't smile, and acts like he doesn't know us.

Nobody believed he was an alien. After watching so many sci-fi movies he was convinced he was a different species than the rest of us. After watching Phantom from Space, he said if he took off his space helmet he would also disappear. After watching The Hideous Sun Demon, he said if he itched his skin enough he would peel away this human costume and everyone would see his real body.

Nobody was a baseball aficionado. He was out on the diamond every night hitting his own pitches and tagging himself out stealing bases. It's a game for weirdos, Nobody said. He wanted chew in his lip, grass stains on his knees, the sun in his eyes. He wanted blisters. He wanted his windup to fool the Great Bambino. He wanted to watch the ball curve with nothing between it and home plate but a prayer. He wanted dirty slides, bloop singles, pickoffs, and moon shots. He wanted to lie in a strange bed next to a naked girl and tell her the only game worth playing is one with a suicide squeeze. He wanted long, boring, extra innings where nothing happens but everything is possible.

Nobody was a riddle wrapped in a mystery chilled in Jell-O.

One night we saw him walking back from the field with his hat and glove, stumbling beside the electric fence that circled the underground military base. There were weird noises and the ground shook and then everything smelled like rotten eggs. Nobody knew what went on out there. Nobody pointed to the barbed wire and said it wasn't actually a fence but the webs of a gigantic vampiric crabantula like in Angry Red Planet. Nobody said he would destroy the hatchlings before they devoured the town.

Nobody unzipped his pants and took a piss. There were sparks
and a crackling and for a moment there were two of him, as if
the world had glitched. Nobody disappeared in a flash of light.

All Will Be Revealed

It is with sadness we communicate the passing of the grocer—found dead in an erotic game gone wrong with his mistress, a synthetic doll purchased from the Kinkalypse— who was just a boy when they built the trestle bridge across the lake. At night, he leaned out the window to watch boxcars rattle through the dark. Like a woolly mammoth herd lumbering in search of grass. He imagined the boxcars carrying candied plums, shrunken java heads, and gold bullion. Sometimes he watched the hobos jump on and off the boxcars. He waved. The hobos waved back. In the summers, he lay on the tracks with the neighbor girl. They kissed. The girl got on a train and never came back. People frequently jumped off the bridge, their bloated bodies washing ashore a few days later, their faces twisted with surprise. When the Mormon prophet visited the town to dedicate the landfill for the site of a future temple, he stopped in the grocery store for the famous spiced rum raisin pudding. An old family recipe, the grocer smiled. The prophet was charmed with the dessert and the grocer convinced himself that if it was good enough for the Lord's mouthpiece then people all over the world would soon come for a taste. He borrowed money from everyone in town to pay for one hundred barrels of sultanas from Iran. But on the morning the train was supposed to arrive, the steel beams groaned, then buckled, and the train hissed steam as the bridge collapsed. A group of fishermen rowed out quickly to search for survivors but never returned. A diver in a professional wetsuit attempted to inspect the wreckage, but after six hours a second diver with superior equipment descended into the lake promising not to return without the first diver. Three days later the mayor ceased all rescue operations. It took years to dredge and drain the lake. They found no train, no boxcars, no fishing boats, and no raisins. Just a pair of lead boots and an empty brass diving helmet with a strange patina. Scientists say it is more than a century old.

The Road Home Ends at the Edge of Heaven

It is with sadness we communicate the passing of the test tube baby whose mother was convinced he'd be the next Messiah. She worked as a motel maid during the day and the night shift at the gas station. On the weekends she taught Lamaze classes in her basement to the pregnant high school dropouts and sold vitamins for the company the FDA later shut down. She dabbled in dog-breeding for a while, but the labradoodle bitch she bought in a Vegas motel died from mastitis after birthing a litter. The test tube boy had a revolving door of stepdads, which he didn't mind because it meant lots of gifts, like the Smiths cassette he listened to on repeat. He was the only one who didn't pretend the cosmonaut boy didn't exist. For a summer they were inseparable. Pissing on the campfire at Boy Scouts and digging for Indian arrowheads in the quarry. They snuck into the country club and took turns putting their dicks inside the jacuzzi jets. They stole a wok from the Chinese buffet which the cosmonaut boy kept looped to his belt and sometimes used as a baseball bat at the park, but his fingers seemed to say it doubled as a sonic pulse cannon capable of incapacitating the aliens from *The Purple Monster Strikes*. They played Battleship during Sunday school whenever the blue lady was teaching. She started every lesson by asking the children to write their names on the chalkboard, not the names their parents had given them but their real name, the one they wanted to be. One girl said she was a cat and wanted to be known as Meow Meow, and a boy said he was a tree and everyone should call him Bark Bark. When the blue lady asked, What is God? one child said, *God is everything*; another said, *God is nothing*; and another said, *God is an old man*. The boys snuck away, cutting through the woods on bikes before squeezing through the chained-up doors of the abandoned ice-skating rink the city council had promised would bring the ice capades and Olympic hockey, not expecting a power outage the night before the grand opening would melt all their dreams. Crossing the brackish water, the test tube boy clubbed the cosmonaut boy with the wok. He stole the pills from his pocket and ripped up the photo of his mother saying she was a real sheepfucker. The cosmonaut boy woke up face down in the mildewed rink water. He stared at his reflection. He limped home in the rain. He watched the ambulance carry away the test tube boy who had been hit by a cement truck and was a blob in the road like a gobstopper that had been licked one too many times. Back home, the cosmonaut boy sat at the table with the pieces of his mother's photo. He clawed at the red patches on his elbows until they bled. You miss your mama, the dentist said. He said he was my friend, the boy's fingers seemed to say. That's the hurt that never goes away, the dentist said, you can get yourself a wife, but it isn't the same. And they leave too. What did I do wrong? the cosmonaut boy's fingers seemed to say. Nobody knew what she was, the dentist said, so I guess it's kind of a joke you only see something once it's gone. Is it the same way on Planet X? People just want to wake you up, the cosmonaut boy's fingers seemed to say. A good woman is hard to find, the dentist said, they've all wised up and left the desert. It's all boys on this pleasure island now, doped up and deaf with religion. The cosmonaut boy scratched the swoosh off the high-tops the test tube boy had stolen for him and, tying the laces, tossed them into the telephone wires.

Light is Like Blood

After a visit to the aquarium, the father found his son on the living room floor pretending to swim through whale veins. Every light in the house flipped on. Light is like blood, the boy said, floating along the carpet down the hallway as he bumped into chairs and tables. Did you know there are whales in the Great Salt Lake with hearts the size of a piano? Sixty gallons per beat, the boy said on the way home from the library, tracing a finger along his veined skin with disappointment. His arms were chubby back then, the scars like train tracks not yet there, white and smooth like Moby Dick's belly. A week later, the house glowed with flashlights and candles as the boy switched between free-style and backstroke. After cutting his lip sleep-swimming down the stairs, he told his father everything about Cetus, the poor sea monster slayed by Perseus, and how Poseidon in his despair arranged the memory of the Leviathan in the constellations. Sometimes the father still finds stray drops in the house. Along a baseboard crack or a smidge on a doorknob. Or there, unbelievably, on the ceiling, the blood he left. The drops are too dark to see with the naked eye. The father turns off all the lights. The drops glow, faint at first, then brighter. He leaves them there, a secret constellation. Stains he can't reach, or won't.

Talk in Song with Tongues of Lilting Grace

The Narrows is the oldest neighborhood in town. The houses are slim and hunchbacked, like teeth crowding a child's mouth. But the sun always seems to shine brighter there, convincing locals it is the best place in town to hang underwear out to dry. A bachelor once lived there in a rundown spite house. He was an RV salesman but told the prostitutes he paid for by the hour at the motel what he wanted more than anything was to compete in the Olympics. He never slept with any of the girls, only fenced. When the prostitutes refused his money, he converted the lawn in his yard into a small pond. He lined the edges with stones and hauled buckets of water from a nearby stream, one by one, until the pond brimmed over the edges. At night he sat near the pond, pleased with his creation. With time, however, the bachelor required more company, so he ordered a pair of exotic toads from a catalog. He painstakingly doted on them until whenever he approached the pond the toads sang. They sang all night, like a deranged symphony, and the neighbors complained they could not sleep. More than once they asked the bachelor to remove the toads, but he refused. In the nature of things, the toads multiplied. Sleepless nights turned friendly neighbors cantankerous until one night, in a fit of insomnia, they massacred the toads and drained the pond. They could not have anticipated, however, retiring to their beds in the weeks to come and being unable to sleep. They tossed uneasily in the silence. They left the radio static crackling. They hummed, murmured, whispered. They read poetry. They prayed. They visited the prostitutes. Nothing worked. A few minutes of sleep at best, but nothing sustained. They longed for the toads and their weird music. But the bachelor had left town and lived in a camper near the salt flats where he had no neighbors and fenced his shadow. His funeral was yesterday. Cause of death unknown.

Sounds Caress My Ear

Every first Sunday of the month, the cosmonaut boy put on the suit he'd stolen from the boutique display window downtown and went door-to-door in the trailer park collecting little blue envelopes from the widows full of tithes and offerings for the church. The old ladies invited him inside for cookies, but he just stood in the doorway. Then he rode his bike past the chapel to the playground at Pill Hill where he sat on the rocket ship and played the accordion. Sometimes the old man with the dog was there. He wondered if the boy looked like the man from Planet X under his helmet, or if he was real at all, and the cosmonaut boy's fingers seemed to say he didn't want to be a real boy like the rest of them, and the old man waved his hand in the direction of the chapel and said better to be a strung-out fool than one of those puppets. The old man had been a blackjack dealer at the Indian casino across the Nevada border before becoming God's postman. That's what everyone called him. He heard voices in his head, or what he said was his brain acting like a strange radio transmitting frequencies to heaven. This is Utah, he told the cosmonaut boy, prayer is our drug of choice. When they found him in the abandoned barn off Highway 21, hanging among salted deer legs like wind chimes, there was a prayer book in his pocket. Bless nana's suspicious mole. Bless lotto numbers 9, 17, 47, 14, 6. Bless Elvis. Bless the water heater. Bless my virginity to be restored. Bless the ice caps not to melt. Bless an 8% return on my stocks. Bless me to miscarry. Bless Bigfoot to find his eternal companion. Bless me to find a parking spot downtown. Bless the dinosaur bones to remain hidden. Bless me to get the vacuum on sale. Bless me to slip on a Slim Jim and get a big settlement. Bless Darwin roasting in hell. Bless this gay away. Bless Deseret Nation to rise again. Bless these teeth to straighten. Bless the moon. Bless these varicose veins. Bless me to get pregnant. Bless the hole in the ozone to get bigger so Jesus can find his way back. Bless the air conditioner to work. Bless the baby in heaven not to forget me. Bless America from the socialists. Bless this gonorrhea. Bless aliens to abduct me. Bless Caucasians everywhere. Bless me to orgasm. Bless this pimple to go away. Bless the enrichment of plutonium to deter our enemies. Bless the dentist across town hunched over the faucet washing out the blood stain in the silky spacesuit stitched together from his wife's underwear as it falls apart in his fingers. Everybody loved God's postman. They tapped on his window late at night wanting their prayers scribbled in his pocket book. They cursed him in the grocery store when he said God didn't have an answer to their prayer yet, and were disappointed when he said he'd spent years tuning out the voices in his head, even trying to have himself committed to the State Hospital where doctors insisted he was unwell but not sick, and what a sin to turn his back on God's gift and get hooked on quaaludes and penny slots and two-dollar ribeyes, they said, but God's postman kept pretending everything was alright even though nothing felt right, and when they asked if he ever said his own prayers he said he didn't pray, he said the last thing I need is to be addicted to clarity.

Watch Out

Around the same time the copper mine leaked arsenic into the groundwater, causing all the babies born that year to have an extra thumb, the anesthesiologist quit his job at the hospital and used the last of his savings to open a small violin workshop downtown. There was a large window where passersby could look inside and see the wood scattered on the floor and half-finished violins hanging on the walls. He lived in the loft upstairs with a band of runaway boys who brought him chopped wood from the canyon and trinkets scavenged from the landfill in exchange for a place to sleep and stories from the operating room. He forced the boys to watch *Amadeus* over and over, telling them they were all unworthy of the sound, when really the boys just wanted to listen to Prince and The Ramones. Watch out for that man, people used to tell the boys, he's funny in the head. The cosmonaut boy used to watch the anesthesiologist work on the violins day and night, his fingers moving fast as if to say it seemed silly to never finish the so-called thing he loved. Art is just as empty as religion, the anesthesiologist said, but we all have to worship something, kid. They found him naked with a plastic bag over his head, death by misadventure the coroner said, which didn't surprise anyone because anesthesiologists are the most unhappy and clinically insane people in the medical field. The violins still hang in the abandoned shop window. On windy days, the sawdust sort of hangs in the air, not quite floating and not quite flying.

Nobody sat next to him at church. Nobody knew what was going on inside that helmet, only that the anesthetic of fantasy never wore off.

Nobody liked Sunday school. The teachers said believers go to heaven, all others go to hell. We learned about light and dark and how it took God seven days to make a garden with snakes and bad fruit.

Nobody said that wasn't true. Nobody said if you walked back in time before glaciers and viruses, back before the big bang and before heaven or hell, there was the desert. Nobody said God must have created the desert from the bones of his father, crushing them into dust and sprinkling them in the darkness. Bewilderness, God breathed into the dead father dust, and it became the desert.

Nobody said God was a mad scientist.

With the leftover bone dust, God made the moon and the stars and had them shine at night because he was afraid of the dark. Then God left, removing all trace of his spirit from the earth and sky, leaving only the echo of his voice behind, what we call the wind.

Let there be wilderness, we whispered.

No, Nobody said, bewilderness.

Snell's Window

To avoid the draft, the tractor supply manager converted to Mormonism and spent two years as a missionary in Guatemala where instead of dodging bullets he preached to drunks and lapsed Catholics, frequently ill with diarrhea, and once held at gunpoint by leftist guerrillas, but spent most of his time translating love letters between the prostitutes living upstairs and their tourist johns. He came home and married a divorced woman with two boys. Before school, the boys found him sprawled on the floor pretending to be the Incredible Hulk poisoned by gamma rays, ripping off his tank top as he flexed. The boys rolled their eyes and ate more cereal. He threw out his wife's wigs but kept the Styrofoam heads after she died, using them to teach the boys the proper way to kiss a woman. He implemented a health regimen. They jogged. They grew aloe vera plants and extracted the gel for weekly enemas. One week they only ate cabbage, the next grapefruit. At night, they swallowed spoonfuls of raw garlic with apple cider vinegar chasers. The tractor supply manager spent a night on NoDoz finishing one boy's book report and the other boy's science project, typing ten pages about what goes on inside a black hole where time slows down and speeds up simultaneously as you're stretched like spaghetti before being ripped in half by the past and future. We are all Rumpelstiltskins, he wrote. The teacher gave it a C+ with a note that said, *Come see me*. He told the boys bedtime stories of when he was a missionary and saw dolphins getting high on pufferfish toxins. The world is a drug, he said, find yours and worship it. His was water. In Guatemala, he dove in rivers and lakes and the ocean and stayed underwater until his lungs almost burst then turned to look up at the refracting light that creates an optical illusion at the surface, a ring, he told the boys, with everything else in shadow. The tractor supply manager stayed up late with the Rubik's Cube, trying to visualize the pattern three steps ahead but found himself always retracing his steps, never lining up the colors, a little like this fatherhood which was always one twist away from making sense.

A Stupid Human Trick

It is with sadness we communicate the passing of the seamstress who fell asleep in the spa tanning bed off Highway 21. The facility remains closed, but the blue neon sign still casts an eerie glow against the mountains. The Renaissance man was the masseuse, manicurist, and hairstylist at the spa, trying to warn the housewives against too much tanning, lying to them that were beautiful just the way they were, but they never stopped talking about their husbands at the KKK rally, and their awful mothers-in-law, and whether their lip fillers looked fake, and how you never fall in love the way you fall in love in the third grade, and about the Mormons obsessed with the singing, the potlucks, the hugs, the polygamy, the handshakes, the pioneering, the Jell-O. Since losing his job, the Renaissance man, who suffered from insomnia, missed philosophizing with the housewives and telling them all the smart things that came into his head, things like, *The future belongs to cultists and voyeurs and quacks* as he massaged their love handles. He drove along Highway 21 picking up hitchhikers. They were addicts and prostitutes and a drifter with hands large enough to crush a bear skull. Another hitchhiker had a terrible sunburn with weepy blisters. At first, the Renaissance man thought he was driving around the ghost of the dead seamstress burnt up in the tanning bed and, hoping to atone for his negligence, kept driving her around town when in fact it was a woman who'd walked three days in the desert to escape a fundamentalist sect she'd joined as a teenager. She talked about how it all went wrong for her after the third grade. That was the best year of her life. She sang the solo in the school play. She borrowed her dad's camcorder and filmed a sci-fi horror romance called *Martianstein* about a lovesick alien who builds a wife out of bits and pieces of Mormon virgins. She won the penmanship contest at the county fair just minutes before the Ferris wheel toppled. All were saved except her mother and five siblings trapped under the debris. Nobody offered to assist as their cries for help slowly faded. They had cut to the front of the line moments before the Ferris wheel collapsed and by deceit, the sunburnt woman said, they earned what they so righteously deserved.

The Gamma People

It is with sadness we communicate the septic man's wife was officially declared dead yesterday on the anniversary of her disappearance. According to the septic man, she went out for milk and diapers and never returned. The septic man went on local television saying she was a Russian spy. He showed the reporter her notebooks full of equations. She'd spent years writing them, scribbling first on napkins and used envelopes, then continuing her equations all over the wallpaper and eventually kneeling for hours scratching numbers onto the floor, like she was praying to them, finding it difficult to stop because eleven smelled like cherries and thirty-three was vaguely homosexual and the square root of sixty-four was sad and right angles felt cold and no matter the equation nine always behaved cuntish, and while she couldn't understand the story they were telling she was seduced by the elegant complexity of math. She didn't even like numbers, the septic man told the reporter. He said it must be a Russian code. But for what? He spent his nights watching grainy footage of the Revolution Day Parade in Moscow, rewinding the tape over and over as he looked for a petite brunette in Red Square with a mole shaped like a half-moon on her cheek, then listened to the dentist next door three whippits deep feeling guilty about not going to church and singing *We're Mormons on the moon/ We have wives by the platoon*, then saying he suffered from a pharmaceutical romance and not an addiction, then saying, I'm tired of people, I'm tired of all their sad little horrors and tired of me for finding them irresistible. He watched the cosmonaut boy's fingers which seemed to say he wasn't allowed back at church after trying to use a Ouija board and microwave to resurrect crickets from the Miracle of the Gulls reenactment pageant. I want to stop looking for proof things won't get better, the dentist said, I want to stop noticing only the ugly things, but I don't know how. The septic man sat at the kitchen table and wrote another letter pleading his case to *Unsolved Mysteries* before putting on his wife's dress and having tea-time with his son who said, You are the dragon and I am the witch, until the septic man's mother came over to babysit so he could go out with another one of the church ladies, none of whom seemed impressed by the numbers scribbled on the walls and floors when he brought them home, nor the tattoo on his penis that said, WE THANK THEE, O, GOD, FOR A PROPHET, in fact it was a turn off, they said, which is why he hadn't gone to college in the first place, because women were fickle but a septic system never lied, and he couldn't understand how his wife could just disap-pear like that, like a number erased from a ledger, just like he couldn't believe that God was a benevolent father but probably more of a clockmaker who gave humans the gift of time because he knew how sad it was to be timeless, but after a while a clock needs to be wound back up except God has abandoned this workshop earth and we are unintended creatures out of sync, and maybe we weren't designed to keep ticking forever, and sometimes the septic man consid-ered there was something the matter with his head filled with so many thoughts, as if God was whispering in his ear, but he couldn't quite say what, or maybe words were just an undiscovered variation of diarrhea.

Nobody traced the path of Russian satellites in the sky. We huddled under the desk for the fallout drill. They were always up there watching, Nobody's fingers seemed to say. Recording everything we did. Like God. Sputnik, his fingers seemed to say. A Russian word that means friend or traveler. Almost the same as spuknyet, *which is what little commie children babble when they're trying to learn the word ghost.*

Nobody told us other things about outer space, but we didn't understand his fingers.

Nobody was sure if he was real. We couldn't tell if he was our sputnik *or our* spuknyet.

There Ain't No Denying

The cosmonaut boy carried off the last seesaw planks. He hammered them with the other wood scavenged from the collapsed barn to replace the charred catapult beams. Bungee cords held tin sheets in place. Two missionaries biked past them into the trailer park. Can you believe that was me once upon a time? the dentist said. Nobody listened to what I had to say back then either. On Planet X, the cosmonaut boy's fingers seemed to say, we don't have conversations with ourselves. The dentist took a whippit and, trying to crawl out of the catapult bucket, fell into the dust. I was never addicted to anything, he said, until I was sober. Nobody can hear you, the cosmonaut boy's fingers seemed to say. It's too fucking hot, the dentist said. He had another whippit. He pissed his pants. It's too hot, the cosmonaut boy's fingers seemed to say, and he reminded the dentist that on Planet X there was only ice and for his assistance he would reward the dentist with an ice castle even better than Superman's Fortress of Solitude. The dentist kicked the rotted catapult beams, You really think this will work? The cosmonaut boy's fingers seemed to say, Do you think they miss me on Planet X? You think like a Mormon, the dentist said, with just enough sense to make perfect nonsense. The cosmonaut boy kept hammering the wood together, ignoring the dentist who said, The thing about Mormons is they're basically football fans, except Jesus is their pigskin. And fanaticism never really goes away, the dentist said, it waits for a window to open then crawls inside and calls it home. It's a squatter. I can't wait to get away from this desert full of idiots who talk in circles, the cosmonaut boy's fingers seemed to say. Use the mouth God gave you, the dentist said, I don't speak Planet X. The cosmonaut boy's fingers moved too fast. The dentist rubbed his forehead and said, This is the dumbest thing ever. Nobody used the seesaw. Not since the girl disappeared. There was a bronze memorial plaque fastened on the middle: *Here lies a strange one who died in a strange way.* The mother used to take her daughter there and they went up and down on the seesaw. Again, again! the girl squealed. That's when the mother taught her the word. *Wiedergänger.* An old word the mother learned from her mother, and her mother learned it from her mother in the old world and brought it with her when she came west to find God in the desert. Say it three times and it comes for you, the mother told the girl. What comes? From her apron pocket, the mother took what looked like an old chicken foot. It smelled of wet tar. Say the name more than three times, the mother said, and you'll be *wiedergänger* too. They went up and down on the seesaw. The girl said the word. One. Two. On the third time the mother blinked and the daughter wasn't there. She looked everywhere. But the girl was nowhere. Nothing but an oily stain in the dirt. The mother had another daughter to replace the one she'd lost. The daughter went door-to-door selling knives, slicing shrimp to impress bored housewives. Late at night she went up and down on the seesaw. She said the word to the dark, but nothing ever came for her. Not boys, not monsters, not God, not nobody. She was twenty-four.

Exit, Pursued by a Bear

We used to get a lot more bears in town. They wandered down from the canyon and sniffed around the dumpsters and maybe took a dip in a motel pool until the sheriff arrived with the tranquilizer gun. Some of them were sold to traveling circuses, others returned to the wild so we could do it all over again the next week. It's strange how some animals provoke fear while others elicit pity. There's something queer about the bear. Maybe it's the way they lumber along thinking vertical thoughts like honey, honey, honey, or how they look so human when they stand on their hind legs. Years ago, not long after the first telephone wires made it to town, the mayor's office set up a hotline where people could call in a bear sighting. But with all the bears hibernating and people being lonely it turned into a party line, a ministry of disappointments we called it, where everyone calls and vents to the operator their frustrations, angsts, and disenchantments. The phone logs, meticulously housed in the local historical society archives, say the local drama teacher used to call frequently. While most believed her fiancé left her at the altar, she claimed he had in fact transformed into a bear to escape the engagement. She promised to marry the first hunter who brought her her fiancé's bearskin hide. Over the years her floor filled with rugs, but none were the lover she was looking for. *Look* magazine profiled her, and she was featured on local television. For a time, she was the most eligible bachelorette in the state. Discovering a malnourished bear cub abandoned by the circus, however, changed her outlook. She trained the bear to be a thespian, hoping it might one day star in a Broadway production of Shakespeare's *A Winter's Tale* in the scene where Antigonus is, comically and tragically, ripped to shreds by a bear. Last week, the fully grown bear mauled to death the drama teacher in her sleep. An audio of the attack was recorded when the teacher phoned the party line. Whether this was an accident, or coincidence, or part of a macabre theatrical performance, nobody knows. After careful reflection, the phone company decided to release the audio recording of the mauling to the public. To spare us the fantasy.

If You Have Any Information Regarding the Whereabouts

Calypsee is a gentle town. Very little happens. This is where highway hypnosis was invented. Where we don't end the pledge of allegiance with liberty and justice and all that crap, but always say *In Armageddon We Trust*. Where lust is common but sex infrequent. Our residents are not quite liars and almost fundamentalists. The majority consider themselves optimistic fatalists. Sure, a runaway child might stab you for a dollar in the alley behind the pizzeria, but he'll say a prayer for you at the hospital and use the money to pay your tithing on Sunday. We are the salt of the earth. Worship is our only addiction. Which is why we could hardly believe it when a man discovered a baby in a ditch where the sewer pipe drains into the river. Its lips were blue and its skin at once pale as a piglet. The man, a so-called sleepwalker who had seen the baby just yesterday at the park unable to hold still, snapped a few photographs of the baby before calling the police. He later apologized for this indiscretion, insisting he only photographed the baby because of its artful pose. The morning after the grisly discovery, two couples came forward to claim the baby. When neither couple could produce satisfactory evidence they were the lawful parents, the municipal council provided each couple with pen and paper and asked them to draw the infant from memory. Photographs of the deceased child were then reviewed in tandem with the drawings. After much delay, the municipality released a statement today saying one couple accurately drew a child, but not the child in question. The other couple did not draw it accurately enough.

There Are Angels Among Us

It is with sadness we communicate the passing of the housewife, a victim of the milk epidemic. It's been all over the news. Beware of tuberculosis. And mad cow. And milkpox. Farmers everywhere blowing their brains out. The apocalypse is just around the corner, reporters say. The pregnant housewife stockpiled: 2%, skim, buttermilk, soy. She studied the cartons with faces of missing children. Doe-eyed, floppy hair, crooked smiles. She invented daydreaming. Aliens abducted them. Or perverts. Or polygamists. Everybody had a theory. It's all a corporate scam, the forklift operator told his pregnant wife, saying the companies got tax breaks if they advertised a public service. The pregnant housewife poured milk down the drain and clipped the missing children's faces into a scrapbook. There's a pattern here, she told her pregnant friends at church. Only children with some names get kidnapped, while others don't. So there must be a safe name, a name that will prevent a child from ever going missing, she believed. She spent all day at the library trying to pick the right name. She drew pictures of what her not-yet child might look like and had extra sonogram printouts made, wondering if the fetal face belonged with the others on milk cartons. She developed strange cravings. Wads of notebook paper and ink from broken pens sipped like wine. She walked into the canyon and ate handfuls of sandstone from the ochre cliffs. It stained her fingers red. Her doctor said every addict believes in miracles and told her to pray away her suffering. Another doctor said it was a nervous disorder. Many women have it, he told her, giving her a vial of pills. Her husband got hooked on them. They kept him awake. That's when they visited him—his babies in heaven waiting to be born. Three of them ready to lose their wings, their bodies fuzzy and blurred, like they were out of focus, he said, but that's how you know it's an angel.

Quaggites from Outer Space

It is with sadness we communicate the passing of the
hydrologist who fell asleep in the Lord on Wednesday
after a brief illness. He was a comforting presence in the
Department of Water Works and a tireless advocate for
local aquaphiles. Married and divorced three times, he
discovered his true passion, the quagga mussel, late in
life. He operated a decontamination portal for boaters
traveling Highway 21. Armed with a special knife, he did
all the hull scraping himself. He admired the tenacity of
the lonely quagga. STD of the waterways, he smiled as
he scraped. No bigger than a thumbnail but colonizing
any surface, stacking atop one another until looking like
casino chips half-melted in the sun. Their sturdy yet deli-
cate shells wouldn't crack under the wheel of a pickup truck
but scratch them on the underside just right and they pried
open. Not unlike a woman, the hydrologist winked. You
can't blame them for being invasive, the hydrologist would
say, are they not also pioneers? While scraping the boat
hulls he'd tell the sunburnt families about the screenplay
he was writing. Extraterrestrial jumbo quaggites who, after
a radioactive accident, wander the galaxy in an eco-friendly
Winnebago until arriving on earth where they release a
neurotoxin into the atmosphere that turns humans into
mindless love slaves. The quaggites then fatten the humans
to harvest their skins into prophylactics to solve the bivalve
overpopulation crisis on their home planet. A dramatic
performance of the unfinished screenplay by the local
high school drama club, with refreshments provided by

the Hindustan Latex distribution center, will occur at
the Ouroboros Theatre on Friday night and double as a
funeral viewing for all interested parties.

Nonsuch Place

It is with sadness we communicate the passing of the psychic, found in the alley with his bleeding head resting on a pillow of broken glass. Everybody loves that alley. A narrow, unlit path behind the shops downtown that looks straight and flat at first glance but actually inclines gradually up thirty-nine cobblestone steps before fishboning into other alleys. Sometimes the alley is not there at all, as if it were a wormhole in the spacetime continuum that vanishes and appears sporadically. People get lost there all the time. They wander around looking for it thinking it will cure their illnesses, or remember the thing they forgot, saying there is no such place like it. The psychic's daughter, a so-called clairvoyant, is often walking around the alley handing out bowls of soup to the homeless, or trying to get the cosmonaut boy to go to school, or buying bus tickets and gorilla masks for runaway girls so they can picket outside the Met and burn pantyhose and the American flag, or rescuing the bachelor's toads from the sewers. She keeps them in a tub above the psychic shop, assuring customers that if they lick one they'll see Heavenly Mother. The baseball boys, who are afraid of women like her with tattoos and lip piercings, call her the blue lady because of her poorly dyed blue hair and the turquoise feather boa she always wears wrapped around her neck. They wander into her shop on a dare, pretending to browse for herbal supplements but really they're looking for a bootleg copy of *The Anarchist's Cookbook*. They pay for tarot card readings with paper route money they didn't tithe to the church. She reads their palms and says cryptic things like, *We are what we worship so open your eyes when praying*, or, *You're not lost, just wandering*. She said the hairs on coconut shells and their milky fluids were proof of our common mammalian ancestor and thank God Eve ate one and got us the hell out of that garden. One of the baseball boys found the psychic's body. He left the theatre in the middle of *Invasion of the Star Creatures* and hurried downtown, past the comic book store and the bicycle repair shop, the smell of cinnamon everywhere, then in and out of alleys until he found the girl on the thirty-ninth step. She wore a leather collar, black eyeliner. She handed him the crumpled note. *Your eyes are crocodile/ scales, blinking heartsick/ arpeggios. Aliens come in twos.* He recognized his cursive letters. You're nothing special, the girl said. She turned to leave but the baseball boy caught her hand in his. On his toes, he kissed her and waited for sparks to fly but when he opened his eyes he noticed the psychic on the alley staircase, the blood under his nose like a moustache, looking up at them. They kissed again, for the psychic, for the last thing he would ever see.

Nobody went to the movies on Friday night for the triple feature. Night of the Blood Beast, Phantom from Space, *and* Devil Girl from Mars. *Death-rays, radioactive fallout, and space vixens.*

Nobody understood sci-fi movies. It was always the same story. It was always the same bad costumes, the same bad acting, the same out-of-tune music. It was always the same naïve wonder. It was always happening in the desert. It was the same people destroying the world so they could save it. It was always platinum blondes fainting into the arms of unbelievable monsters. What were they trying to sell? Nobody knew.

Nobody was obsessed with sci-fi movies. He worshipped them. He loved the illogical stories. He loved the grainy footage, the amateurish camera work, the awful props. He loved the foolhardy scientists and the damsels in distress with bullet bras. He loved the hardboiled men smoking cigarettes. He loved the fifty-foot women and the forbidden planets. He loved the weird lighting. He loved that in a black-and-white sci-fi film the quantity of chest hair is directly proportional to chances of survival. He loved the melodrama. He loved aliens pretending to be humans. He loved how you never really know somebody even when you know them. He loved how in a sci-fi movie everything is true and everything is false and nothing is impossible and everything is probable because in the desert conspiracy is your gospel. He loved the optimism, the madness, the dread, the delusion, the obsession, the erotic tension. Nobody loved how in sci-fi movies the world was always ending, but always beginning too. Nobody loved their cheap stupid beautiful paranoid sappy weird pulpy hysterical atomic belief.

Nobody stayed for all the credits. He loved how a sci-fi movie got stuck in the haunted screen of his brain. How he caught himself pacing a room like Dr. Cadman in The Black Sleep, *or waking up in a cold sweat from a noise that was the same noise the alien parasite made in* It Conquered the World. *In the desert everything is a ghost machine, Nobody's fingers seemed to say, but maybe I escaped from a movie, maybe the ghost is just me.*

Nobody exchanged his mother's old pearl necklace for a bicycle at the pawn shop. Eventually, the bicycle will sink in the quarry and he'll tell everyone it was the aliens from planet Zemar who stole it, but for now he rides. He doesn't stop at the end of the street, or the end of town, or the end of anywhere. He pedals past alfalfa fields. He rides past a dead fox on the highway and a man slumped in the alley with a needle in his arm. He rides past the salt flats. He sleeps in a dumpster where flies are his only friends and his fingers seem to tell them he will not go back, they seem to say there is no home, they seem to say dead things should be given a key so they can unlock the bodies they've been locked out of. And the flies buzz. And the tire skids leave a curve in the asphalt like the echo of a black hole. And the stars are like a drug that beckon him to the next desert and the next and the next. And in the next town they invite him into the chapel. We love you, the worshippers say, but only if you leave, and in the next town the worshippers say, We love you but never come here again, and they say the same thing in the next town, and the next, the towns all like salt and the chapels all like dust, and the stars blinking as if to say to be light you must first explode. He bikes into starlight. Nobody can stop him.

Time is a Cosmonaut

It is with sadness we communicate the passing of the taxidermist who started collecting roadkill as a boy. He didn't play sports. He didn't sing in the church choir. He didn't join the Boy Scouts. He was never invited to birthday parties. His parents had him baptized twice, just in case. He woke up early to collect highway roadkill. He brought the dead animals back to the basement and dissected the bodies, learning how to carefully strip away the skins and craft them into taxidermied mounts. Instead of flipping burgers like other teenagers, he taxidermied the pets of grieving old ladies. He was never sure if he was bringing the animals back to life or killing them all over again. He didn't win a prize at the science fair the first year he submitted a staged diorama of taxidermied rabbits playing croquet, and not even the following year when he created a scene of frog Americans and toad Nazis at Omaha Beach. It's just wire and string, he told the confused judges. By the time the taxidermist became the city coroner he had his own art gallery downtown with his Frankenstein creations: angelic squirrels with pigeon wings in a Nativity scene, and foxes signing the Declaration of Independence, their posed faces unstuck from time. Many in town called him a pervert, especially after he was excommunicated from the Mormons for having a vasectomy, chastising him for preferring the company of dead animals to his estranged son, but those of us who knew the taxidermist found him a gentle, God-fearing man whose one wish was to work in the Department of Resurrections in the afterlife. He looked forward to reassembling the beetles he'd melted with a magnifying glass, and the crickets he'd grinded into paste on the sidewalk. The taxidermist died Thursday last of leukemia believed to be the result of constant exposure to embalming fluid and the arsenic used in his taxidermy mounts. His gallery will remain open. We encourage friends and neighbors to contribute to the roadkill photo album as the situation allows, and when running over raccoons and possums on the highway please smile and think of our taxidermist up in heaven putting back together all our mistakes, our accidents, our fits of quiet menace.

In the Very Least, a Ghost

When the bus driver looked in the mirror, he saw a little girl inside him. Chic bob haircut and black drop-waist dress with a lace collar. Like a ghost from a 1920s speakeasy. Nobody else saw her. It's just your guardian angel, his mother assured him. For years, the little girl scribbled away in a notebook. 3:57 a.m. Urinated in bed. 7:22 a.m. Lied about spilling juice on newspaper. 7:36 a.m. Lodged raisin in nostril. 11:44 a.m. Smashed cricket with rock. 2:11 p.m. Licked laundry detergent. 4:04 p.m. Dislodged raisin with sneeze and consumed. 8:28 p.m. Prayed for forgiveness for smashing crickets. 8:36 p.m. Masturbated. 8:44 p.m. Prayed for forgiveness. 8:49 p.m. Asleep. The guardian angel was not very helpful. She gave the bus driver wrong answers on the math test in the fifth grade. A few years later she let him fall off the roof and break his arm. She lied and said the enemy was reloading. She said smoking doesn't cause cancer. She said the cosmonaut boy had AIDS, so the driver kicked him off the bus. All the guardian angel wanted to do was dance. At the rodeo bar, the bus driver ordered bees knees and highballs. For the girl, he told the bartender, who always gave him a funny look. You have one too? a stranger asked him one night. He was a fireman. He also had a little girl inside of him. The soul of a girl he was supposed to save someday, he believed, or maybe the one he couldn't save. The fireman's little girl had taught him all about fire. How to burn ants with a magnifying glass. The history of Alexandria's library. London. Dresden. Chernobyl. Don't believe the reflection in the mirror, the fireman said, telling the bus driver all the invisible things nobody else sees—that's who you are. My love is like to fire, and I to ice, the bus driver said. The fireman smiled. They grew old together. They died within a few hours of each other. They say two women in black dresses place fresh flowers on their graves each Sunday, but nobody has ever seen them.

*Nobody said the desert is a mad place. Nothing grows here
except dreams. It is a place for wanderers. Nobody lives here
who wasn't born a nomad. Swedes, Danes, Norwegians, Scots.
Immigrants running away from famine and poverty. Running
away from other lives. They dreamt of a place called Deseret, the
land of honey, and like bees they wandered from home too far
and followed the voice of God west into Utah. Here they would
no longer be nobodies. They would be pioneers. They would be
saints. They would be prophets and visionaries.*

*There's a word the German immigrants brought with them to
this Utah desert. Wiedergänger. They said it in the old world
but didn't understand it until they converted to Mormonism.
Wiedergänger. It doesn't translate well. Traveler. Ghost. Pioneer. Zombie. One who walks again and again. Not as simple as
a resurrection. A soul who comes and goes. A necronaut, slipping
between this world and the next and the one before and the
one sideways, moving in loops, like a soul stuck in a doorway,
a soul orbiting its own obituary. It's one of those Grimm things,
those children's fables people assumed stopped being true after
we leached uranium from the earth and lost the need for stories
because reality is too radioactive. Wiedergänger. The pioneer
thing that walks and walks and refuses to die. Cut off its head
but it just grows back. Change its name but it finds a way back
from the past. Like a rumor. That's wiedergänger.*

*This all happened after the war. It was a time of babies and
suburbs. A time of crew cuts and gadgets and the perfume of
sex in the air nobody could smell. The golden age of black and
white. There were no poets. There were no plagues. There were*

no spies, or dust, or ecstasy. There were no new wars, or fear, or paranoia. It was a time of handshakes and Cheshire cat grins. Nobody was a cripple. Nobody was an alien. Nobody was lost. Nobody was gay. Nobody was forgotten at the parades, the picnics, the school plays, the Sunday morning sermons. The air was sand and salt. It was a time of rumors and rumors of rumors.

Nobody's ever done an autopsy on the anatomy of a rumor. How they lodge in the throat, small and knotted and gnarled. Cut one open and it's full of spindly fibers. Layer after layer. Like a womb. They dissolve upon touch but leave a sticky sensation on the skin, because a rumor will always outlive a fact. Say its name and the wiedergänger will come for you. There are polygamists next door. That's Wiedergänger. *The Mormons invented television. That's* Wiedergänger. *See that* sputnik *in the sky? They are spying on us. Who are they?* Wiedergänger. *God speaks to prophets in the voice of a white salamander.* Wiedergänger. *There are men living on the moon dressed like Quakers.* Wiedergänger. *Blood atonement.* Wiedergänger. *Kids who grow up believing* Plan 9 From Outer Space *is a documentary?* Wiedergänger. *Africans are the children of Cain?* Wiedergänger. *Cain is still alive only now we call him Bigfoot?* Wiedergänger. *Yoda was inspired by the prophet?* Wiedergänger. *Oh, you're a relapsing Mormon?* Wiedergänger. *Is it true there's a boy wandering the desert with a fishbowl on his head trying to catapult himself to the stars?* Wiedergänger. *There's no hiding it. There's no denying it.* Wiedergänger, Mormon. Mormon, wiedergänger. *What's the difference? It's part of our soul. Buried in there, undead, waiting to wake up like Sleeping Beauty. All Mormons are* wiedergängers. *It's in our blood, what keeps bone fastened to muscle. Wiedergänger is what hides in our fat. Wiedergänger is what keeps our mind and our tongue and our bowels in constant communication, because shitting and talking rely on the same principle. Dead things never go away, they always walk again, always orbiting, always dying so they can be reborn and if you haven't figured that out yet then you've been* wiedergänger *for a very long time.*

Piano, Unblinking

The piano was in the parlor gathering dust. When anyone tried to play it the keys wouldn't sound. Only when they left the room would it play properly, a faint melody like raindrops tapping against the window. Our haunted piano, the family told guests. After coming home from the war, the youngest boy, a decorated soldier with shrapnel in his chest, would sit in the parlor and stare at the piano. He knew if he left the room the ghosts would start playing. He'd seen many of them during the war. Ghosts and pianos, but mostly pianos. The Air Force started parachuting them onto battlefields to boost troop morale. He would play and sing before a battle, then play and sing after a battle. By the end of the war, things were going poorly for the enemy whose airplanes started dropping pianos when they ran out of bombs. When they ran out of pianos, they dropped zoo animals. Elephants and hippos and zebras. They floated through the sky, wailing. The soldier's friends, who had avoided bombs and bullets and trench foot for so many years, were crushed by this strange new music. Once home, the soldier became a recluse and refused to leave the parlor and stared at the piano, unblinking. Last week, they moved him to the bed upstairs hoping to calm his nerves, but it was music, not decades-old shrapnel, that killed him.

Not Quite Floating, Not Quite Flying

Recently, the crane operator admitted under oath it was not an accident when the nine-thousand-pound wrecking ball snapped from its cable and tumbled down Mangrove Street, injuring dozens and killing three as it pinballed against cars and shops and curbs before its odd turn into an alley where it almost crushed a cat but, thankfully, only pinned the feline's tail under its weight—it was a deliberate sabotage, the crane operator confessed. The crane operator, who had received two previous restraining orders for stalking one of his victims, claimed an angel had appeared to him confirming the young woman, an actress, was in fact his wife and the two had been married in a previous life and foreordained to wed once again on this earth, thus, he insisted, he had no choice but to sabotage the wrecking ball to prove his love and then marry her in the temple by proxy after she was dead. Almost as soon as the tragedy was over, news resurfaced that the deceased actress had returned from Hollywood a few years ago where she had a small part in the unfinished John Wayne film, *Beau John*, and had kissed the Duke so, naturally, rumors started that since the wrecking ball had crushed the actress it must have touched her lips which, essentially, meant the wrecking ball was John Wayne's lips. Men come from all over the state to kiss the wrecking ball and take photos with it. It looks sad, covered in grime and graffiti, as if wishing it could still be tumbling somewhere else. The cat tail is still there too. The cat, its tail pinned under the wrecking ball, yowled for days until someone notified the dentist who for years had doubled as the veterinarian and on occasion still treated animals, which he preferred to people, and he swiftly cut off the tail and brought the animal home. He named it Waffle.

Pathologically Charitable

The only truly haunted place in Calypsee is the railway station just past the salt flats where last week a train collided with a drove of wild horses. The force of the collision was so devastating that, rather than mangling their bodies, the horses evaporated on impact into a pink mist. The cosmonaut boy was sitting on the tracks sending a distress signal to the mothership on his ham radio when it happened. Just as the last echoes of frightened whinnying faded, he watched as a cowboy, who during the week visited classrooms mesmerizing students with pockmarked arms and handing out D.A.R.E. frisbees, rode down the slope. After a few minutes, the cowboy gave up trying to lasso the pink mists and wept furiously.

Drinking Alone Beneath the Moon

The speedway is abandoned now, a graveyard of engines and tires and rusted car skeletons. The secretary of the local John Birch Society built it with the settlement he won from the radon gas leak at the duplex. He was out there every weekend looping around the track with only the sheep to race. He'd won the flock as part of a different settlement against the rancher. Love the thing that bites you, he said, showing everyone the scar on his hand. It was one of those Dugway ewes the Air Force poisoned with VX gas, somehow still alive years later. The speedway man kept her penned up in the track with a wild goat and bred lambs over and over. Within a few years he had a feral flock. The ones that weren't stillborn had bigger heads but shrunken faces. They grew extra teeth. Their tongues were black instead of pink. Their fleece turned bluish and knotted like briar. They hardly moved unless it was to eat or fornicate. When the speedway man died out on the track of a heart attack, the mongrel sheep ate him. Then they ate each other. The dentist and the cosmonaut boy found the mess. They'd come to work on the catapult and found it a heap of ash and twisted metal. How many times is this now? the cosmonaut boy's fingers seemed to say. They say the Salt Lake Temple spires are actually UFOs, the dentist said, maybe we could handshake our way inside and hijack one of those. They notified the sheriff. The cosmonaut boy moved his fingers fast. What's he saying? the sheriff wanted to know. Sorry, the dentist shrugged, I don't speak Planet X. He your kid? the sheriff asked. The dentist laughed. No, he said, I only wish I was from Planet X. You two a couple of beatniks, is that it? the sheriff said. More like a freakshow and his unemployed guardian angel, the dentist said. You think this is some joke? the sheriff said. Nobody's laughing, the dentist said. Shouldn't he be in school? the sheriff said. He's got nowhere to be, the dentist said. You do something to this poor kid? the sheriff asked, why is he wearing that thing? Nobody knows, the dentist said. The sheriff started pulling on the coils and hoses trying to remove the helmet. If you take it off, he'll turn invisible, the dentist warned, trying to hold back the boy from kicking the sheriff in the shins, or maybe he's got that new radioactive brain eating parasite inside there, the one the government is experimenting with underground, and if you take it off it'll let loose a night of the blood beast that'll infect everyone in town with happiness. The sheriff handcuffed the dentist. Not really necessary, the dentist said, I got nowhere to be. No mothership, no aliens looking for me. Talking with you feels like being lost inside a whale song, the cosmonaut boy's fingers seemed to say. They watched the sheriff circle the track with a shotgun putting down all but one of the sheep monsters. It rode with him in the patrol car scaring the bejesus out of people. It wasn't mean and nasty and bleating at its own shadow, but kind and gentle and even cuddly. The sheriff had never married and had no kids. Every morning the sheriff fried scones. He sold them to the bakery downtown. His secret ingredient was the milk of the blue sheep which he drank straight from the udder. Everyone else used store-bought milk for their scones, but it wasn't the same.

Like Sorts Inside a Dream

It is with sadness we communicate a small retraction is in order for one of yesterday's obituaries. It was originally reported a woman married some thirty-seven years died following the Ferris wheel collapse at the fairgrounds. In the chaos of that accident, she suddenly found herself in a hotel room, deceased, naked with a man not her husband and reviewing the afterlife manual of instruction. The woman turned to the entry on INTERCOURSE. It read: *Go forth with confidence. Be fruitful and multiply and replenish this sphere to fill the measure of its creation.* Her not-husband removed his pants and stood like the figure in the illustration. Together, they inspected the not-husband's pubis. It was totally void of genitals. Just a smooth mound of skin. The woman's pubis was equally smooth and hairless, like a plastic doll. Maybe we missed something, the not-husband said, shaking his head as he flipped through the pages of the manual. Let's read it again, the woman suggested. Originally believed to be dead when pulled from the wreckage, the woman has since made a miraculous recovery.

Nobody fell in love with the crick-neck girl. She wasn't born with her head bent like that. She started bending it after listening to the bishop at church. There are angels among us, he said from the pulpit. She imagined them floating above her and from then on her head went crooked.

It'll get stuck like that, her parents warned, half-teasing and half-worried, but by then it was too late.

The crick neck-girl led Nobody through the field, guiding his hand over the leafy tips, educating him in the sex life of alfalfa. She crawled through the window of the abandoned train station. Nobody followed. They watched the boxcars pass from one side of the desert to the other.

They're like lost elephants, Nobody's fingers seemed to say.

You talk funny, the crick-neck girl said as she rubbed his fingers.

I speak in moons, Nobody's fingers seemed to say.

They lay in their underwear on a dirty mattress. She played with the coils and latches on the neck ring, trying to pull off his helmet so she could look in his alien eyes, but he just thumbed pages of the flipbook he'd drawn.

You're not going to take it off, are you? she said, tracing a finger over the cracks in the space helmet. Her eyes were an intense green, like the sky before a tornado. I can't, his fingers seemed to say, the helmet was the only way to protect himself from the brain eaters. *They'll never like you, you know that, right?* she said.

Nobody's fingers seemed to say, I have a doomsday heart and can resist the temptations of any fire maidens from outer space.

You don't know anything, she said, *you're just a boy.*

He knew she was disappointed that without clothes he wasn't the alien she had imagined, just like he was disappointed she wasn't like the wild women of Wongo. He took a bump of Special K. His body slumped like an unused door slipped off its hinge. It was a whippit. That's what his mom used to call it. That weird feeling as if the heart stops and snaps like a whip at the same time. He'd been chasing that feeling all his life. God. Pills. Movies. Boom. Nobody fanned out his fingers to mimic an explosion.

You ever seen an alien? she asked. A real one, not that angel shit they talk about on Sundays.

Nobody thought of Zetha, the mute princess with hair like raven feathers adrift on a phantom planet waiting for him to find her.

The crick-neck girl stood at the broken window daydreaming about how she'd grow up to be a bartender, stopping knife fights and marriage proposals like they were one and the same, refusing all the barflies but not the poet from the big city passing through town. He'd tell her to put on a black dress before taking her to the fancy restaurant and watching her drink wine even

*though she hated the taste of it. He wouldn't laugh when the
crick neck girl showed him all the poems she'd published clipped
from the newspaper, even read them aloud in his raspy poet
voice so she would slip off the dress. She'd recognize her words
a year later when she bought the poet's new book, her feelings all
gussied up like a well-polished turd. The crick neck girl wouldn't
know whether to be mad or sad, so she let out a big broken laugh
that boomeranged from the future all the way back to the train
station where it woke her up from her daydream. What do you
think happens in the future? she asked Nobody.*

*There are aliens all around us, Nobody's fingers seemed to say,
only nobody is looking.*

Compassion

It is with sadness we communicate a young girl being treated at the Utah State Hospital for Melancholics and Other Incurables bid adieu to the earth and its scenes on Sunday morning with perfect resignation. She had been committed by her mother who informed the doctors her child displayed no interest in the toys available in her nursery that the mother had purchased brand new, choosing instead to play with the broken, deformed, and otherwise infirmed toys the young girl salvaged from the landfill. It disturbed the mother, such compassion for things not real.

Stockholm Syndrome

After the bank security guard watched *Invasion of the Saucer Men* during retro night at the Ouroboros Theatre, he went searching for his daughter on the so-called lover's ravine where teenagers often park to engage in kissing and some light petting. Forcibly opening a car door with steamed windows, the security guard began savagely beating the boy he suspected of ruining his daughter. Much to his disappointment, the security guard realized the boy was alone and, to impress any passersby, had created the illusion of romance inside the car by filling it with a dozen hot pizzas. The security guard, embarrassed by this pitiful sight, offered a terse apology for messing up the boy's face like a dirty dinner plate and continued searching for his daughter. After this awkward encounter, whenever the security guard saw steam—in the shower, or rising from the manholes outside the bank—he felt aroused. And whenever his wife attempted intimacies he craved a slice of pepperoni pizza with black olives. Months later, his daughter eloped with the pizza boy who she had started dating to spite her overbearing father, the two of them high on ecstasy while robbing the Pizza Palace. The manager was shot in the scuffle and died of his wounds after three agonizing days. The judge gave the pizza boy twenty years for pervading the innocence of a minor. The girl got six months of rehabilitation at the School for Misfortunate Ladies, even though she pulled the trigger.

In Our Lovely Deseret

It is with sadness we communicate the passing of the pharmacist's widow, a truly remarkable woman who handed out candy to the children and cocaine lozenges to the baby-fevered housewives, once even saving a boy's leg after a wood chopping accident turned it yellow with gangrene by using a salve of coyote urine. You can cure anything with coyote urine, she used to say. She had few friends and wasn't invited to sit with the other widows in lawn chairs near the highway and place bets on which crows scavenging roadkill would be run over by big-rigs. Sometimes one of them might say, Polygamy probably wasn't so bad, or, squinting from the sun, It's so fucking white here. But she had dozens of lovers. Men are a drug, she told the bored housewives at church, only the dose makes the poison. She was eulogized yesterday by the town drunk, her closest friend. Everyone called him the one-arm bandit because he played the slots at the Indian casino across the border. Most nights he hitchhiked out to the old Narco farm hoping to get clean with some quaaludes and jazz, but then remembered it had been closed for years after the roof collapsed, and the clinics and halfway houses always told him there was no room and he'd have to sober up elsewhere. One morning, we found him passed out in a driveway, but nobody had the time to help because we were already late for church. It was the widow who shooed away the turkey vultures chewing on his face. She stitched his mouth back together as best she could, but he never talked right after that, always mumbling, even when he gave the widow's

eulogy, telling the congregation what the widow had told
him about her boy, her only boy, and how after he died
she'd gone to the World Scout Jamboree in Austria wearing
his nametag and uniform and wandered around the old
camps still ringed with barbed wire fences and heard foxes
yipping. She came back to the cabins and described the
sound perfectly, mimicking it even, saying they were arctic
foxes, a very rare thing, but nobody believed her, the scout
leaders saying everyone had been awake but nobody else
heard it, that this wasn't the kind of place where foxes
say goodnight, that it was impossible, really, correcting
her memories by saying that arctic foxes were scavengers
who wouldn't wander this far south. She'll always be us,
the town drunk mumbled, but nobody knew what he was
saying. Not that it mattered. The Mormons didn't like the
drunk. He told too many stories. His father fell down a
mine shaft before he was born, and his mother died in
childbirth. All he had were stories. Not ones he imagined,
or ones God gave to him in a vision, but the town lore. The
historian, people jokingly called him. What really bugged
them, though, was a drunk Mormon was almost like a real
person, with real feelings he didn't learn out of a hymnal,
and when he was drunk he wandered like he didn't mind
where he might end up and that terrified the Mormons
who thought life was a Bingo game and one day God is
going to call your number. The bishop never looked him in
the eye, those wet drunk happy glassy miserable eyes. Not
long after the pharmacist's widow passed the town drunk
died too. The death certificate says he died of remembering.
It was his only talent.

Sure as the Dust That Floats High in June

It is with sadness we communicate the passing of the church organist whose funeral, after he threw himself off a cliff while hiking, was poorly attended. The organist had only recently awakened out of a coma of some nine years, a miracle, the doctors said, but almost immediately after regaining consciousness he became irritable, insisting something was off, as if he was the wrong color of paint in a family portrait, feeling as though he was living in the wrong time and wrong place. I'm homesick, he told the doctors, who said you can't be homesick when you're home, but the organist said he was homesick for the home he was in. Eventually, he started remembering what it was like being in the coma and came to believe that the so-called coma was where his real wife and his real children lived in the real world, but this so-called life he had awakened into was actually a dream world with an impostor wife and impostor children. He could tell by the dust. In the desert there's dust in your hair, dust in your eyes, dust under your nails, dust sticking to your skin right after you wash it off in the shower. But here the dust was phony, the organist said, and eventually he couldn't take it anymore and threw himself off the cliff. Don't be fooled by all the love-bombing, the dentist whispered at the funeral. The cosmonaut boy's fingers seemed to say, If you had one out to get in the ninth inning, who would you go with? That's how they get you, the dentist said, Mormons kill you with smiles and handshakes. I can't decide between Goose Gossage or Rollie Fingers, the cosmonaut boy's fingers seemed to say. They fool you into believing this is just a desert, the dentist said. The cosmonaut boy's fingers seemed to say, I'm growing a horseshoe mustache like Goose Gossage. I've got five generations of dust here, the dentist said. On second thought, the cosmonaut boy's fingers seemed to say, give me Lee Smith. Nobody's hitting that sleepwalking motherclucker. Dust sings, the dentist said, it sings come fertilize this burning orchard of rotted fruit. A portrait of the organist hung inside the chapel near the bishop's office alongside the portraits of all the previous bishops, and the cosmonaut boy—who came to the funeral because the organist was the only one who believed the boy was an alien and said the way he played the accordion reminded him of the real world he was trying to get back to—recognized the dentist's portrait before he was bald as an egg and wore glasses. The cosmonaut boy tried to imagine his own portrait on the wall but couldn't remember his face. He knew if he removed the space helmet he would slowly turn invisible, like the alien in *Phantom from Space*, so he sat in the pew beside the blue lady and wrapped a finger around her turquoise hair and she traced a finger down the crack in his helmet to where the rubber rings were fused to his collarbones. I bet you're hiding some wild, saintsick eyes in there, she said. He showed her the sketches in his notebook for the trebuchet he was going to rebuild to launch himself toward the mothership. She told him, Hope is a drug, my little donkey, it can give you wings or hollow you out like a bowl and then someone pours all their dreams into you, warning him not to get hooked or he might end up like the church organist homesick for a real life.

Misbelieving

Someone wrote on the gas station bathroom stall the paramedic sodomized a monkey as a missionary in Africa and that's how he got AIDS. They included a phone number. The hospital fired him. His landlord evicted him. Nobody shook his hand at church. His father, who always said there was nothing worse than being a fag, dropped dead from the shame. The paramedic moved into the motel. It was the same motel where the cosmonaut boy, before all the motels had Magic Fingers vibrating beds for a quarter, rented himself out to Mormon teenagers. The teenagers lay naked on one side of the bed, the boy perfectly still inside the girl, and the cosmonaut boy shaking the bed as the teenagers soaked inside each other guilt free. It's the future of love, the cosmonaut boy's fingers seemed to tell the man at the hardware store where he bought more wood for the catapult. The paramedic's only friend was a possum that came nightly to scavenge the dumpster. He named it Snuggles. He rubbed two greasy pennies together as he told Snuggles about his father's funeral. One penny with a scuffed side, the other shiny. His father had stolen them from the fountain downtown many years ago. One for his pocket, and one for his son's pocket. Sometimes they sat around imagining what people had wished for. Misbelieving, his father called it. The paramedic had taken the penny from his father's pocket after they laid him out in the coffin. The funeral home forgot to put shoes on his feet. One sock had a hole in it with the little toe poking out. His grandmother saw it and said the dead never stop walking. She said they wear out their shoes following the sounds of their names, saying the afterlife doesn't really exist so the dead go memory to memory in the heads of those left behind. Hollow out your head so your father has a place to call home, the grandmother said. He's always been living there rent free, the paramedic said. The paramedic woke up hungover and found a dead possum in the parking lot. Distraught, he borrowed a shovel and dug a grave in the woods behind the motel. Some of the other guests, moved by his compassion, brought punch and gas station chicken wings. Halfway through the eulogy, the real Snuggles suddenly waddled across the parking lot. Crying turned to cheers and a celebration for the return of Snuggles.

Green, Like the Sky Before a Tornado

It is with sadness we communicate the passing of two baseball boys, twins, who fell down the old pioneer well during a game of hide-and-go-seek. They were eulogized by their Sunday school teacher, the blue lady, who recently confessed to the cosmonaut boy there is a species of copulation she envied. Not the arachnid who cannibalizes her mate. Or the honeybee who explodes his genitals in mid-flight coitus. But the snail. A genteel lover, she said. She liked to watch them surface in the grass after the rain, the glint of their spiral shells in the sun as they circled one another in a strange diplomacy. They're hermaphrodites you know, she told the cosmonaut boy, one body with two minds. The dentist told the cosmonaut boy to stay away from her, that she was a weirdo and a thief. At night he watched from the window as the blue lady undressed and the secrets spilled out of her clothes: wedding rings, a slice of uncooked bacon, cemetery flower petals, a piano string, a single red satin glove, three spider legs, a tortoise shell comb. But her favorite was to steal snails from the aquarium. He told nobody. Because on Planet X snails were spiritual creatures, not like the radioactive slugs in *The Monster That Challenged the World*. Because all neighbors are perverted in their own way. Because, his fingers seemed to tell her, when you're friends with a thief you long to be the thing they steal next. He needs a mother, the blue lady told the dentist, a woman's touch. The dentist, who hadn't slept in three days thinking the boy had disappeared again, told her, You're no mother, you'll ghost him

like everyone else. You have your ghosts, the blue lady said
gently touching the wedding ring on his finger, but I got
nobody. In the kitchen, the snails disembarked from the
blue lady like dazed refugees and roamed the countertop
in their tantric confederacy. She explained to the cosmonaut boy how one snail fires a harpoon, spearing his mate
through the neck. Slouching away, he thinks fatherhood
is so easy but then the other fires a harpoon of her own,
impaling him, their jellied bodies now corkscrewed, him
and her, sexing and unsexing in this old labyrinth of intercourse. She melted the butter. The cosmonaut boy minced
garlic and parsley. They watched the snails bubbling in
wine, their grey bodies curling deeper inside the shells.
She pried one loose with a fork and dropped it down the
cosmonaut boy's mechanical hose. It's a sophisticated taste,
she said, licking her finger. The cosmonaut boy shrugged.
The best, she said, is when they stew in their fear down in
the shell, down in that pocket. The world is just pockets
inside of pockets, she said. Some things trying to find a
pocket, others trying to be a pocket. Crawl out of one and
you find yourself in another. Like the poor baseball twins
down the well. To get out of a fairy tale you have to fall
up the sky, she said, like a raindrop in reverse, one world
down by going up. There's no way out but deeper. See?
They taste better when they hide and you have to pull
them out, the blue lady smiled as she denuded the snails
from their shells. See? And she pulled him closer.

Nobody waited for the mothership. Every night he'd climb the water tower and, like a real cactus brain, send a distress signal on the ham radio using the fishing pole as an antenna. Once the mothership found him, his fingers seemed to tell us, everything would be different. Back home, his alien friends would let him play baseball. He'd walk in his real skin out in the sun and it wouldn't itch. Everyone would hear his voice.

Nobody walked everywhere with that fishing pole. He never caught anything. Except once. It was at the lake far out beyond the salt flats. After reeling in the fish, he watched it flop in the sand. Its mouth wriggled. Pulling on the line, the fish coughed up a stone. It was flat and oblong, spackled with glittery pits. Nobody said it was a meteorite.

Nobody rummaged through his pockets and found a lemon drop. The fish swallowed it before darting back into the brackish water. A fair trade, Nobody said.

Nobody looked at the meteorite in his hand. It was warm. He skipped it across the lake. A few minutes later, the meteorite skipped back. He put it in his pocket and kept walking.

Cheesemongering

After the Air Force decommissioned the missile silo, the SFC still went to work every morning. He kept all the equipment clean and ran the generator every four hours just in case. He updated the ledger. He took the proficiency exams once a month. He put up warning signs with big red letters on the fence to deter trespassers. During the graveyard shift he told himself the story of the night the young airman accidentally dropped a wrench down the launch tube and, ricocheting, it exploded a fuel tank but miraculously not the warhead. The SFC imagined himself reduced to a little charcoal pyramid. To stay awake, he converted the bunker into a cheese cave. He cultivated the bacteria himself. He salted, molded, soaked, wrapped, and bathed the cheeses in a light brine. He measured their temperatures. He watched them age. He thought of himself like Samuel Pepys, the great diarist, burying a wheel of parmesan while London burned. In Sunday school, he gave lessons on emergency preparedness. He made colorful posters with diagrams for rotating canned tuna and dehydrated milk. Opening up a fifty-pound sack of wheat, he sifted the grains through his fingers. He displayed his firearm. The ratio of bullets to grains should be equal in order to survive the Second Coming, he told the congregation. When the Air Force found out what he was doing, they court-martialed him and confiscated the cheese. He got a new job at the hardware store but could not recover from the loss of his cheese, which felt as if his children had been kidnapped. He died in a house fire that started in the basement when an electrical outlet ignited tins of peanut brittle. He was forty-nine. His estranged wife taught middle school. Around the same time the Voyager probe orbited Neptune, finding nothing but clouds and ice, she ran the fallout drill simulating a nuclear attack. Huddled under their desks, the cosmonaut boy fooled the blind kid into believing the Russians really were invading. In the panic, he was hit by a car in the street, distracting everyone long enough for the cosmonaut boy to steal a sextant from the principal's office. The SFC's estranged wife changed her name in the phone book. She cried reading to the class the end of *Where the Red Fern Grows*. Later, she burned down the post office for flying the flag with the blue bars and stars in honor of the old Deseret Nation. She died, suddenly, of complications arising from a romantic game in which the bishop, who informed authorities he had only visited her to administer a blessing, misplaced a banana in her fur purse. Voyager headed into deep space.

All I See Turns to Brown

The pomegranate tree that dropped rotted fruit into the dentist's yard belonged to the neighbor, a florist, who imported the seeds from Jerusalem because she believed the Utah desert could not be the promised land in America without the pomegranate. Every morning, she used an old insecticide pump to shower the tree with her urine. She went door-to-door giving away the pomegranates by the bushel, but nobody knew how to eat them, so she had a special hooked knife she carried with her to carve the pomegranates in the doorway, placing the red seeds on outstretched tongues while reminding neighbors this was the forbidden fruit in the Garden of Eden. The dentist found the florist naked beneath the pomegranate tree one morning, her face swollen and purple having ingested two quarts of pesticide. Just the day before she had knocked on the door carrying the cosmonaut boy who had passed out in her orchard. You're pretty bad at this, she told the dentist. Yeah, well, he said, they assigned all the real devils to Salt Lake, so, he's stuck with a lowly apprentice. They'll take him away, she said. That little hopeless hope is all I got right now, the dentist said. The dentist carefully dressed her corpse in some of his wife's old clothes, but the paramedics told him he shouldn't have done that, that it interfered with their work, and he watched from the window with a kind of déjà vu as they loaded the florist into the ambulance, noticing the glass had thickened at the bottom window edge, surprised to realize glass is not a solid but a slow-moving liquid that drips down over the years, pooling into a thick mottle at the base until it cracks. The dentist moved around the kitchen slowly. It had been years, but he still cooked for two. He watched the dust storm. He remembered when the desert felt magical. Now, everything was pale and stressed and thin. He wanted to stop watching but couldn't. The power went out. He lit a candle and watched the moths spiral closer and closer to the flame. A fat one landed on the wick. Its body flickered, then wilted. It was over in an instant. But somehow the dentist kept thinking about it long after, remembering the way the wings moved with a clarifying bewilderment before disappearing, remembering how his wife once told him only the female moths are attracted to fire and only after they've laid eggs, but the dentist wasn't sure he believed that, and maybe they weren't attracted to the flame so much as disoriented by it. We should go to church, he whispered. He rubbed the embroidered initials on the yellowed pocket square and tried not to think about the tiny spasms of life inside him. They give you one of these in the temple, he told the cosmonaut boy, to wave at God during the end of the world. He held it to his face and huffed. The cosmonaut boy muscled a bump into his thigh. He swayed. His knees buckled. On the stairs he twitched like a wingless bee. Stay with me, the dentist said. He put his hand on the space helmet to keep it still. The boy sort of pulsed on the floor. Nobody said anything. Later, the dentist swept up the moths wilted into balls of string under the window, comforted by the fact that it seems so easy to disappear but really isn't. Stuff gets left behind.

As the Sun Burns the Ground

Sheep bleat in the distance. The streets look like dark tourniquets bandaging together the scarred desert. The gardener clips a hedge. The stenographer slips yet another curse word into the official courtroom transcript. The jeweler fixes a watch, anxious he has added more time to a world already spinning out of control. The cosmonaut boy wobbles dopesick beside the groaning boxcars on the railroad track on his way to the playground. He sits on the tire swing as the blue lady slips a bottle of pills into his pocket before swinging him higher. Later, after they've scavenged the landfill, the cosmonaut boy and the dentist follow the old Paiute road trying to remember where they've hidden the catapult. Either we're lost or the Mormons burned it down again, the dentist says. Nobody will find it, the cosmonaut boy's fingers seem to say. It's the pioneer addiction, the dentist says an hour later, walk and walk and walk. And when you're not walking read your scriptures, can those peaches, say a prayer, smile at the potluck, make babies, feed the missionaries, make soap, move a neighbor's piano, sell vitamins or wrinkle cream or Tupperware, rescue a cat, baptize your dead. Did you know Dodger Stadium is built on the ruins of the Chavez Ravine Sanatorium, the cosmonaut boy's fingers seem to say, and on some days you can still smell the tuberculosis in left field? You better get back to that mothership soon, the dentist says, before you too start believing busy is the same as living. Fucking Dodgers are a disease, the cosmonaut boy's fingers seem to say. They see the weatherman walking home after a long day of distributing EPA comic books on the Indian Reservation. The latchkey kids these days are not really interested in Gamma Goat warning them to avoid the abandoned mine shafts. Already they've fled to the sand dunes to drink stolen beer and set off fireworks and watch the sun disappear behind the sandstone cliffs like bloody milk curdled in a skillet. Like other men who lost their jobs when the uranium mill closed down, the weatherman does what he can to make ends meet. He runs an illegal weather station from the trailer park, broadcasting a nightly radio show on speculative weather in the area. Reports of fertility fog and euphoria rain and carnivorous wind. Hail that turns everything into glass. Snowsqualls that induce sleepwalking and lightning that causes amnesia. *Beware the pogonip* is his sign-off. His headless body will be found in a few weeks, followed by a spell of unweathering. No clouds, no breeze, no rain. Just sun that seems to eat a hole through the sky. Everything pale and still and white and too hot for the eyes. But for now, he waves to the cosmonaut boy and hands him a copy of *The Misadventures of Gamma Goat*. He is fifty-three.

And My Eyes Fill with Sand

It is with sadness we communicate the passing of the butcher boy who got his job the day after he turned nine. 4:00 a.m. twice a week transferring the deliveries to the freezers. Some of the meat slabs were bigger than him. He came home with fleshy guts under his fingernails and smelling like soured gravy. Butcher boy, the kids at school teased. He never complained. He graduated to linking sausages. By the time he dropped out of school he was manning the counter beside the master butcher, a man he considered his real father. Even then he was wearing the parachute. A World War II T-5. If anybody asked, he lied and said it belonged to his father who paratrooped into the Dresden firebombing on some days, and the jungles of Okinawa on other days. He wore the parachute as a precaution. Think of it as an insurance policy, he told a woman on their first date, in the event of the Rapture. All those people twinkled up to heaven—there's bound to be a stray gust of wind. She declined to jump off the water tower and test it with him. Another woman said on their date he talked about underground missile silos and took her to a uranium mine shaft in the desert where he got low to the ground and said something like, Can you hear what's coming? It was carbon monoxide, not Armageddon, that killed the butcher boy. After the Hoffman bombings made national news, neighbors said the butcher boy locked himself in the house fearing the deep state would soon take down the church, then knock over the rest of the government dominoes. He stockpiled bullets.

.22s, .45s, .223s, .357s, .38 specials, and .50 BMGs. He lined them up on the shelves in his house. His wives, he called them. He bought more. Lugers, birdshot, buckshot, and slugs. Fat ones, skinny ones, hollow points, open tips, 12-gauge. He had Soviet bullets, gook bullets, and Uncle Sam bullets. Enough for every pinko commie plus the aliens. Some bullets like a big sassy gin-drinking woman, some like a needle-nose pencil dick. One that could even take down an elephant. Is there an elephant problem in Utah? the neighbor asked. As goes Utah, so goes America, the butcher boy whispered through the mail slot. They found him seated under a window lotus-like with a shotgun and tin of potato pearls in his lap. His thumbs hooked in the parachute pull ring. All his life dreaming the wrong catastrophe.

Reach, or Won't

It is with sadness we communicate the passing of the gym rat who died Sunday after falling from the oil pumpjack. It was a game the kids played. Black Gold. Shotgunning beers while riding the pumpjack as it see-sawed. He was a true believer, and although his body will be given over to the cool lap of earth his memory lives on in each of us. So said the gym rat's father who was in town for the funeral. He gave the eulogy bleary-eyed, telling the congregation he spent the night terrorized by fleas in the motel. They bit his ankles, his chest, behind his ears even. He chased them across the carpet before finally catching one with a pair of tweezers, but in his grief could not bring himself to kill it. Instead, he told the flea about his dead boy. His boy for whom the gym was a chapel. The father confessed to the flea he regretted not speaking with his boy for many years, just as he regretted his ruined business and walking out on his marriage. The father went out to the pumpjacks to watch their rhythmic see-saw. Oil bubbled up from the dust. Behind the pumpjack was a billboard near the highway. The original had been erected decades ago by the Mothers Against Devils Society with an image of a bearded man peering through the clouds with the words JESUS IS WATCHING YOU. The billboard was later graffitied by teenagers who painted Jesus green with antennae and warned of an impending alien invasion. THEY'RE COMING. The new advertisement was for the Christian sex shop. Alien Jesus had been repainted once more into a smiling, anthropomorphic dildo with the caption: HAVE

 The gym rat's father watched horrified as the cosmonaut boy straddled the pumpjack as it rocked back and forth. What if he falls? the father asked the small crowd holding candles at the vigil, but the bishop told him not to worry, that it would be easier to baptize that boy after he was dead.

The Cranium is a Space Traveler's Helmet

After the school kids watched the *Challenger* explode on TV, the science teacher went around the room and gave each of them a drop of mercury to play with. They held a memorial at the flagpole the next morning. The local poet laureate, who wrote mildly pornographic poems about alien housewives seducing fathers away from their families and the Army contaminating the water supply causing widespread erectile dysfunction, said the prayer. The cosmonaut boy stitched together the dentist's wife's silky Mormon underwear into a spacesuit while watching news footage on loop of the rocket boosters zigzagging a Y-shape vapor plume across the sky like an autopsy incision. Smoky bits of spaceship rained from the sky over and over. The dentist took two whippits and wondered if the astronauts fell twelve miles out of the sky at 9.8 m/ s^2, or maybe miraculously they were launched out of the atmosphere into orbit at 17,000 mph, obit or orbit, who knows, or maybe there is a God and they evaporated in the explosion. Are ghosts real? the cosmonaut boy seemed to say with his fingers, and the dentist said ghosts have it easy, the world just passes through them and meanwhile he had to figure out whether to brush his teeth or put his head in the oven each morning. The cosmonaut boy's fingers moved faster as if saying, Is your wife a ghost? The dentist crushed the pills and mixed them with warm water and heated it in a spoon until it turned into a blue goop like a melted Smurf, pushing the needle under the boy's skin and pulling the plunger slightly until a spurt of blood coiled in the tube like a red sea horse. Hold still, the dentist said, time to flush a riddle in your vein. The boy went limp. Later that night, the dentist was a chaperone for the sleepover at the school library for kids who had memorized the periodic table. They ate pizza and told dirty jokes. You can see me, right? the dentist asked the science teacher. And you can see him too, that little retarded kid with a space helmet? Tell me I'm not imagining him. The science teacher scrunched his brow and asked if this was some kind of trick. Sometimes I worry he's not real, the dentist said, like he's my ghost, my demon. Like I'm the crazy one and everyone in town is in on the game. Seems like the most Mormon thing possible. Do you need some help? the science teacher asked. My wife always said it would happen, the dentist said, said my brain would snap and I would be punished for thinking too much. I figure he's the kind of hell I deserve. The science teacher, whose mother was a QVC addict and eventually killed him for the insurance money, got drunk on fireball shooters and told the kids how he had applied to the Teachers in Space Project and never married but frequently donated to a sperm clinic. I have a whole family, he told the kids with a wave of his hand, somewhere.

Rosabelle, Believe

For three dollars the locksmith's commercial on television promised, *We'll open the heavens in thirty minutes or your money back!* He cut keys but preferred to wow customers with a Houdini lockpick he'd won at a magic convention in Boise. One summer, he ran a promotion for non-Mormons offering a lifetime of free services if they came to the Carnival of Life extravaganza. The entire chapel was transformed inside and out into a fairground. Visitors were corralled booth to booth winning either gold or grey tickets depending on the game. After an hour, the only way out of the game room was to present the tickets to the locksmith who guarded the door wearing a white robe and fluffy beard scavenged from the Nativity box. He informed each player that the makeshift fairground was a metaphor for life and some games had given holy tickets as a prize and others worldly ones. Depending on which games they played and which tickets they won would determine their eternal reward. He then led husbands and wives and children to their appropriate afterlife room. Those in the lowest rung of heaven were locked in a room without air conditioning and given Oreos without milk. Those in mid-heaven received angel food cake with no paper plates or cutlery. Those with a sufficient number of golden tickets went to the celestial room where they took off their shoes and ate banana splits. And those with worldly grey tickets were locked in closets, alone in the dark, eating Devil's Food cake. One husband who was locked in a different room from his wife later found her with a certificate saying she'd been married off to a Mormon man along with four other women. He broke the locksmith's nose in the parking lot. Over the years, the locksmith got a lot of death threats. Rumors circulated. That he was an escaped Nazi. That his wife used to be a man. That he'd summon Houdini with a Ouija board. That hidden among the keys in his shop was a master key that fit right behind the ear and could unlock everyone's head in town. He promised after he died to come back and share the secret for getting into heaven. They found him face down under the old trestle bridge. The river had been dried up for almost a century, but the autopsy showed water in his lungs. How do you drown in the desert?

Nobody is an alien, we told Nobody.

We fooled him into crawling inside a hollowed-out log saying it was one of those radioactive zombie trees in From Hell It Came, *and if he crawled in one end and out the other he'd time travel to his home planet. Once he was inside, we rolled it down the ravine. Nobody wobbled out, bruised and bloodied, turning in circles.*

Another time we told him if he spun in circles fast enough, he'd spin right out of his skin, freeing his brain to float back to Planet X. He got so dizzy he stumbled into the street and was hit by a car.

Even then, Nobody didn't make a sound.

Nobody didn't belong in the desert, we said. The West is our dream. Hoboes like him were ruining our wilderness. Do you know what happens after the end of the frontier when all the maps are finished and all the cities have names? The men get jukebox brains and barbershop hearts, we said. Their hands go soft. Their eyes look like ashtrays. A VCR soul. The man without frontiers has a phone booth for a church, wears a hand-me-down suit meant for a joker but thinks he's a superman unaware he's living in the wrong story, running out of dimes as he syncs his soul to the dial tone drone. He can't look a stranger in the eye. Can't pick up a spare in the bowling alley. Can't leave the toilet seat up in his mailbox marriage. Always two minutes late for the bus, skipped over for promotion. He just missed being great. He's patient zero with a civilization fever, we said, and lice make nits.

Nobody's fingers seemed to say, You're space children and you don't even know it.

We broke his fishing pole. We ripped off his stupid cardigan. We smashed the jar and grinded Syzygy, the decapitated chicken head, into a yellow paste. Fuck the future, we said. Fuck radio-active telepathic crabs. Fuck brain eaters.

We pinned Nobody on the ground and put firecrackers down his oxygen hose. We told him he wasn't an alien, just the bastard son of a dopesick mother. We told him to say something. Anything. He moved his fingers slowly and softly. Somehow it hurt having no idea what he was saying.

We kept kicking. We kicked him until we felt real, until nobody made a sound.

Dreamsick

Last year, an aging father looking to get rid of family heirlooms gifted his daughter an antique sardine fork. At first,
she was indifferent to the crude little utensil but quickly
became enamored with it. She frequently polished it,
sharpened it, even carried it in her purse to the theatre
and gatherings for M.A.D.D. Late at night she lay in her
bed, her mind racing with thoughts of the fork: the sound
it made skewering a sardine, or the unspeakable pleasure
of the prongs rubbing the inside of her cheek. She hosted
tea parties where all they ate were sardines. Broiled with
lemon and thyme. Sautéed in butter with shallots and
olives. Grinded into a pâté. Poached. Raw. Neither her
children nor her husband appreciated her refined palate,
worried she was seized with a mad addiction of sorts.
Months later, live imported sardines from mail-order
catalogs arrived. Monstrous things with bulging eyes and
lopsided jaws, their scales shiny with an orange film. She
stacked them in jars and kept them in the attic. Unsatisfied
with the catalog service, she arranged the marriages of
sardines, breeding them until the toilets and sinks in the
house overflowed, the floors slick with brine, prompting
her children and husband to storm the attic and smash
the jars. Slowly, the woman recovered her sanity. Recently,
she unexpectedly found a jar hiding under the floorboards.
The tightly packed sardines had dissolved into a greasy jam.
The woman cried, but whether for the sardines or herself
she wasn't sure. Death by sepsis, the coroner claims. She
was forty-four.

Caution: Men in Trees

It is with sadness we communicate the passing of the city manager who, before he met with a fatal accident yesterday, had been spending his days removing road work signs. Bright orange ones fastened to telephone poles. CAUTION: MEN IN TREES. The kind of sign he'd seen a thousand times before and never thought anything of it. The first night he saw one he got out of the car and looked around. The street was empty. But he felt something ominous he couldn't quite explain. He put the sign in his trunk. A duplicate sign appeared a week later across town near the school crosswalk. He checked the schedule. There was no tree maintenance. He asked the workers and they just smirked, as if they thought he was trying to trick them. The signs kept appearing. He went door-to-door asking residents if they'd seen men in trees, but they looked at him as if he were crazy. He started throwing the signs into the landfill, the cheap orange paint rubbing away and staining his fingers, and once he even burned the signs, but this did nothing to stop their multiplication: on bus stops and in alleys and attached to old chain-link fences. He drove the signs past the salt flats to where the desert stretched out like a geological circumcision and he found the dentist and cosmonaut boy tying together ropes for the catapult sling. The contraption was fifty feet high. This is insane, the dentist said, but what the hell do I know. Reason is for fairy tales, kid. Be mad, the dentist said. Be dreamsick saintsick lovesick homesick brainsick truthsick. You'll grow up soon enough. Had they seen men in trees?

the city manager asked. Cluck off, the cosmonaut boy's fingers seemed to say. The city manager returned home and, just as he was removing his trousers to use the toilet, noticed a single orange crayon balanced upright on the seat. It was the exact shade of orange as the signs. He rubbed the crayon between his fingers. He tried to wake up his wife hoping she could explain this menace, but she rolled over mumbling. Over the next few days other orange crayons appeared: under the church pew, inside the city manager's hat, on the bus, floating down a street gutter, even in a spoonful of his wife's lasagna. She laughed and said the children were playing a prank. He didn't understand the connection. Why trees? Why crayons? Why orange? The doctor prescribed him valium. First the crayons stopped. Then the signs. The city manager spent days patrolling the city thinking about them, strangely missing them. He flushed the valium down the toilet, but neither the signs nor the crayons returned. He stopped washing his hands, even, afraid the orange stains would disappear too. Late at night he lay in bed listening to his wife breathe. He stood in the yard in his pajamas trying to spy men in trees. Crawling back into bed, he debated whether the city council would let him burn down all the trees in town and imagined the orange flames. He struck a match and watched it flicker out. Maybe they'll come back tomorrow, he whispered. What happens tomorrow? his wife asked dreamily. Nothing, he told her.

Rapturitis

It is with sadness we communicate the passing of the aerospace engineer who lost his job after the *Challenger* exploded. He tried to reenlist with the Air Force, but they disqualified him on a technicality. He had nine mouths to feed. He started working at the dog food factory. His boots glistened after each shift with pink slime. The first few months the family lived off their food storage: tins of potato pearls and dehydrated tuna. On Sundays, the engineer and his wife clipped coupons together. They pawned heirlooms. Most nights, after a meal of microwaved Spam and instant rice, his wife watched syndicated episodes of *Alfred Hitchcock Presents* while the engineer stayed up late listening to Art Bell on the ham radio. During the week, he used license plates for target practice. At Christmas, he cut out pictures from the toy store catalog of all the things the children wanted but he couldn't afford—bicycle, He-Man figurines, Rainbow Brite doll—and put them in home-made frames which the children hung on the walls. Then the engineer slit his throat. He was thirty-nine. The neighbors collected money to give the children a real Christmas. But the children seemed confused by this gesture and let the baseball gloves and Barbie dolls mildew on the lawn. Casseroles and clothes met the same fate. At night, we'd see the oldest daughter with enough hairspray to put another hole in the ozone sneaking out of the house. At church, everyone said it was sex or drugs or both, but really she just rode her bike to the aerospace plant two towns away. She hid in an arroyo while the scientists tested rocket boosters. Standing in the burn pit when it was over, she grinded her heels in the char and inhaled the residual toxic fumes until it tickled her throat, watching the sunrise and thinking how she'd rather be anywhere but here, and yet she could not imagine being anywhere but here. The next day at school the teachers played reruns of the *Challenger* explosion on the television. They paused and rewound the tape over and over. They assigned more homework.

The Crawling Eye

She moved into the neighborhood one summer, a pious girl, or maybe she'd been living in the house all along and was just one of those ghosts who, like a friend's extra pinkie, you suddenly notice after a long time. At first, the baseball boys thought she was a prude, kneeling under the tree every night to pray. They spied on her all summer through the fence slats, listening to her prayers, waiting for her skin to lobster after sunbathing and hoping she would invite them one by one to rub her down with aloe. It was only then, up close, that they noticed her glass eye. She never said what exactly happened. If it was an accident, or whether she was born that way. The baseball boys never asked. They were hypnotized by that sexyweird glass eye. She kept it on the nightstand facing her while she slept so it could watch over her all night. She had the baseball boys polish it. They were devoted servants now, addicted worshippers of the glass eye. Do you think I could be one of them? the cosmonaut boy's fingers moved fast. Don't ever be one of them, the dentist said. Do you think I can make it to the Hall of Fame with my knuckleball? the boy's fingers seemed to say. I think you can't be crazy forever, the dentist said. All the great ball players have nicknames, the cosmonaut boy's fingers seemed to say, so maybe they'd call me Puss-in-Cleets because I have a way with words and my windup looks like a cat scratching fleas on a tightrope. The dentist told him to please be quiet for once in his goddamn life, then apologized for his bad heart, saying whoever gave it to him found it on clearance and nobody told him how it works because the instruction manual was in a foreign language. In the nature of things, the eye was stolen. The baseball boys looked everywhere for it but no luck. The girl's father took her to Salt Lake City where a jeweler fashioned a custom glass eye just for her, but it wasn't the same. The baseball boys stopped coming, loitering around the pharmacy instead and stealing nicotine gum which they took turns wedging up their assholes for a ten-minute buzz. The praying girl stopped praying. The tree withered. Eventually, she put her head in the oven. Can't blame her, the dentist told the cosmonaut boy, saying she was a nobody without that eye and that feeling eats you up over time. Every now and then someone will come to the pawn shop saying they found a glass eye in the sewer, or a dog dug it up at the park. It's always a scam, but for a moment we become believers again, overcome with that sexyweird feeling, our happiness tightening as if in a vise.

Good Evening or Good Morning As the Case May Be

After his affair with the aerobics instructor, things went poorly for the podiatrist. The IRS fined him $20,000. He had to borrow a rifle to put down the family dog. He swaddled all the pipes as if they were baby Jesus, but they froze and burst anyway, flooding the basement. He was fired from the community theatre production of *Fiddler on the Roof*. He lost feeling in his fingers. His wife drove the Volkswagen to Idaho and never came back. On birthdays, he got a card in the mail from his son wishing him dead. The woman at the nursery warned the podiatrist not to plant the three holly bushes too close together. They're gossiping gals, she said. Sure enough, they grew taller and thicker. He invested the last of his money in a mail-order machine that reads the thoughts of plants. When he turned it on it gurgled then hissed smoke and never turned on again. He never knew if the bushes were really bad-mouthing him and saying he was no better a father than his old man and a lousy lover too, or maybe even spilling secrets about the Beirut bombing being an inside job. He spent all day watching reruns of international chess matches. He was convinced it was only a matter of time before Bobby Fisher emerged from hiding to take down Boris Spassky and end the Cold War once and for all. That's what the bushes are gossiping, he called in to *West Coast AM*—Bobby Fisher's coordinates. He heard rumors that someone who fit Bobby's description was seen in Budapest, then Reykjavik, then Salt Lake City. Even after they hauled the podiatrist away

to the State Hospital where he taught aerobics lessons
until slitting his wrists, we listened to our bushes at night.
They grew taller and thicker, their pollen a strange shade
of yellow sticking to our fingertips. We knew it was only
a matter of time before the grandmaster showed up here.

Nobody knew why the bishop walked with crutches. It was his idea to build the water tower to prevent the Russians from contaminating the water supply. We have to keep ourselves pure, he always said from the pulpit, spirit and fluids.

Sometimes we saw Nobody up there playing his accordion. His legs dangled off the ledge. From there we could see the white marlstone cliffs ringing the town that sat in the valley like at the bottom of a toilet bowl. Nobody's murky fishbowl helmet rocked back and forth as he watched the sheep foraging near the uranium waste pond. Their fleece glowed blue.

Sometimes water leaked from the tower and there was just enough of a puddle to make a watery mirror in the dust. Then Nobody would sit next to the puddle and stare at his space helmet head inside the moon's reflection, like rings inside a tree. He traced his finger around the circle. Nobody knew if he'd ever seen his own face, or whether the helmet was just empty. Nobody knew if he was a fiend without a face whose brain floated around town at night. It was the golden age of brains. Brains sold as souvenirs in a Money, Mississippi drugstore. Slices of Einstein's brain on a bus tour. Brains on fire at the Surf Ballroom. There was no brainwashing. There were no lobotomies. Amnesia had not yet been invented. Nobody had seen all the brain movies. Alien brains, reanimated brains, and disembodied brains hypnotizing the milkmaids and beatniks. Brains free-floating like aerial jellyfish, but mostly bottled in jars and glass tanks as if put there by housewives, because mad science is always close to home. In outer space it's never about hearts. It's always a carnival of sad awful lonely brains far from home, monstrous brains scheming to the sound of a theremin that makes a noise like someone unzipped a star and inside was a drunk choir boy drowning in electricity. The brains keep coming. They invade earth again and again for revenge, for love, for someone to listen to their telepathic thoughts. They look like old meat patties left in the sun. They pulse. They glow. They fall apart so easily.

Even though he built the water tower, the bishop never climbed up there. He was afraid of heights. Up there, the desert stretched out like a film strip and every day a single frame developed, the light separating from the darkness, the blurs coming into focus, the years getting wound into a reel. Only God should have a view like that, he said.

You look like something that crawled out of the Old Tooele Poor House, the bishop liked to tell Nobody. We knew a girl who got locked up there, he'd say. She would sit under the tetherball in her wheelchair at recess feeding sugar to stray lizards. Then during geometry she took them out of her pockets and pulled off their legs. They never made a sound. She'd cup them in her hands and give them a blessing same as the elders did for old ladies on Sundays. And sure enough, we'd come to school the next morning and their legs had grown back. Nobody believed it. But we believed it. The elders didn't like it. They asked her all sorts of questions, like how she did it, and why she had the gift, and even told her it was unnatural and to stop doing it, but she didn't listen. Her parents were dead so off to the poor house she went. Made it so she could never have kids like her. I remember them wheeling her away in the middle of class, the bishop said, she had this look on her face, like she'd fooled them, like she wanted them to take her away, like out here everything was always being reborn, everything coming back for more, a real nut house of miracles. The bishop said, That was the winter after the winter I started believing I was believing. Once you start nobody really stops believing, the bishop said, believe me, nobody does.

Pilot of the Storm Who Leaves No Trace

Sometimes we still think we see the aviatrix flying above us in her crop duster, a pioneer in the first and only aeronautical epoch in Calypsee. They tried to put her in dresses and pearls and make her carry umbrellas, but she loved grease and boots and sky. Youngest of six daughters, she was always climbing trees, quickly graduating to rooftops, then the water tower, and finally the cliffs. The only way out is up, she told her sisters who thought she was crazy. Never been a sane woman make the world turn, their mother sighed. The first flying contraption she assembled was a dirigible powered by a dozen hot air balloons. Everybody laughed even as she disappeared into the clouds. Fifty-seven minutes later she returned. The crowd expected stories of queer birds of paradise and heavenly streets paved in gold, but the aviatrix told them other than a toothache the trip was uneventful. It's all empty space, she said, just wind and silence. Nobody believed her. She used to fly in circles over the salt flats. The rumor was there used to be an old Paiute city out there surrounded by a field of calypso orchids when the conquistadors came searching for gold and converts. The Paiutes went to their tents and prayed to their gods for deliverance and were turned into salt. Flying at night, the aviatrix said, she could hear the drums beneath the salt crusts. When they finally came to commit her to the nursing home, she convinced them to let her have one last flight in her crop duster. The plane was never found. The cosmonaut boy built his space capsule in the aviatrix's abandoned airplane hangar, cobbling it together from old refrigerators and the occasional NASA satellite scraps that crashed in the desert. He was always doodling in a notebook. Never letters or words. Just hooks and spirals and loops. We never imagined he'd actually build something that was just as strange as the spacecraft from *The Gargon Terror*. He welded everything into a giant metallic orb, like a misshapen testicle. Inside was a nautical helm attached to a bicycle for flight navigation. Along one wall was a constellation map, the rest cushioned with egg crate foam. The ham radio sat atop an old school desk. Once he flipped the switch, his fingers seemed to say, the mothership would come for him. If all else failed, he told the dentist, he could use the sextant to navigate. He painted SYZYGY in bright red letters on the door. The dentist helped him rebuild the trebuchet to launch it. They found the design in the library. This will never work, he told the cosmonaut boy whose fingers seemed to say, Believe in something even if it's wrong. You're a weird little shit, the dentist said, you don't really believe you're an alien, do you? The cosmonaut boy's fingers seemed to say, Queen Aelita says to do the impossible you have to try the absurd. They hauled the trebuchet out to the salt flats. They were going to do a test flight with a cantaloupe but ended up launching the cat. The cosmonaut boy hated cats. He said his mother had been one of the *Cat Women of the Moon* who fell in love with an astronaut who left them here in the desert to go back to his other family. The cosmonaut boy greased the channel before inspecting the pivots and counterweights. He waited until the dentist was two whippits deep before swapping out the cantaloupe in the launch bucket for the cat. It yowled. He pulled the lever. The wood groaned and the springs squealed as the arm swung. The dentist brought his hand to his eyes to block the sun. Well, he said, there goes Waffle.

Life on Kolob

It is with sadness we communicate an accident at the military base claimed the lives of four persons today. Names classified. Regrettably, the dentist—who cleans teeth pro bono—was not among the victims. Nobody knows what the military is doing beneath all this dust and salt. Rockets, pesticides, psychopharmacological agents destined for some Russian village. Maybe cooking Special K for the blue lady. Kolob, we call the base. In honor of that distant star mentioned in Mormon scripture where God has a timeshare laboratory for making all his creations. Our Kolob is surrounded by barbed-wired fence with armed guards at every post. Maybe they're trying to number every grain of sand in the desert to make a weapon out of it. Why else would the scriptures say, *I will multiply thy seed and thy sorrow as the stars of heaven and as the sand which is upon the shore?* On occasion, we've spied the scientists emerging from the bunkers around midnight. They take turns doing cartwheels, as if trying to signal to God at his telescope hoping he'll intervene down here. It looks simple, but the cartwheel is one of the more mysterious human inventions. Hands on the ground, back straight, glutes tight, body inverted in a sideways rotation. But the cartwheel is a dangerous thing. There's always the possibility you get stuck upside-down halfway through. Or just keep spinning. Or time goes in reverse when you land back on your feet. More than likely, you'll crash into a fellow cartwheeler, like those galaxies a million light years away tangling together. You can see them with the telescope at the observatory. The galaxy with two cartwheeling rings: the outer band of swirling stars spinning counter-clockwise, and the inner ring of stars spiraling clockwise. Once merged, the galaxy is held together by thin spokes of cosmic dust and radiation, unsure if it wants to keep spinning or abort itself. After a failed cartwheel, the scientists lie there awkwardly with swollen elbows and bruised hips, gasping for air and wishing away the pain, wondering whether the hand that twirls the galaxies is the same hand that winds us up to watch our aborted play, wondering why the desert is full of happy accidents both pointless and vital, full of so many things forbidden, out of reach, unknown.

Cosplay

After his son died rappelling in the canyon, the fumigator enlisted the local Indian Guides youth group to help him scatter the boy's ashes on their weekend campout. Once a month, the fathers and sons painted their faces and wore headdresses and faux leather vests during a wilderness pow wow to earn achievement patches in fishing, hunting, tracking, weaving, storytelling, and other survival skills, giving themselves new names like Big Chief and Little Chief, or Big River and Little River, and roasting marshmallows around a campfire talking about John Wayne and the Donner Party. The dentist begrudgingly joined the other fathers and sons only to find himself separated from the rest of the group as he and the cosmonaut boy looked for a rock where the boy could carve a picture of his mother. The dentist watched the cosmonaut boy crush Mormon crickets under his heel. There used to be a lot more of those, he said. They'd come in the summer and devour entire alfalfa fields. Then the government sprayed VX gas that left everyone with a mad ringing in their ears. I don't miss them, the dentist said, telling the cosmonaut boy the universe is just a messy dinner plate and we're undigested hors d'oeuvres the Big Bang belched out that were never meant to exist. They wandered through sagebrush. It rained. They took shelter under a juniper. Dizzied by the perfume and unable to find their way out of the canyon, they pitched their tent. The dentist woke up hours later to the sound of the cosmonaut boy prancing around with a rubber enema tube dangling from his naked butt and an empty vial of Special K in the sand as his fingers seemed to say, I'm an angel! I'm an angel! Within minutes, the ketamine had scorched his rectum and he evacuated his bowels, the two of them taking turns soaking up the hallucinogenic diarrhea off the sleeping bag and huffing it drop by drop in a paper sack. The Indian Guides, meanwhile, had also gotten lost even though the fumigator had hired a Paiute from the reservation to take him on a spirit walk to find a suitable burial ground for his son, recalling for the group how he and his dead son had been Big Bear and Little Bear many years ago, but this was the source of their bitter relationship and he wasn't sure whether the boy's rappelling death was an accident or out of spite. The Paiute, who could see the dust storm coming over the bluff, tried to convince the fathers and sons to head back to camp, but they were whooping and howling and crawling on all fours trying to summon the spirit of Little Bear. During the storm the dead boy's ashes were swept away with the wind. The group was rescued two days later, almost dead of heat stroke and dehydration. Not very good Indians, the Paiute told paramedics.

Father of the Four Winds Fill My Sails

The baseball boys spent the morning throwing pennies down the sinkhole. They used the phone at the library to prank call the AIDS Hotline. They watched scrambled porn on the basement TV, their breaths slow and synced. They rode bicycles up the canyon and back. They hit fly-balls and played pickle. They took refuge from the sun in the bowling alley and practiced 7-10 splits. They drank warm Pabst. The pinsetter machines were glitchy so the retired therapist who owned the alley was always in the ball pit behind the lanes in case anything malfunctioned. The boys found him fisting a pistol. Two bullets. Just the other day he had reported to the city council that a Russian submarine had infiltrated the city's sewer system. Armed with maps, the therapist insisted the submarine had wandered off its patrol from the Gulf of California up through the Colorado River, then following a course north-north-east through the Virgin River and up the Santa Clara and Magotsu Creeks before, inevitably, getting stuck in the Calypsee sewers. It's only a matter of time, he said, before the distress signal pings its way back to Moscow followed by a self-destruct order which could level the entire town. The council voted unanimously in favor of reconnoitering the sewers. Three sanitation workers returned from the excavation with no credible intelligence of whether there was or was not a Russian submarine. The body of a fourth worker, severely bloated, was discovered a week later in a runoff drainpipe near the creek. After the funeral, one of the surviving sanitation workers got hooked on benzos but instead of helping him sleep he stayed awake all night watching *The People's Court.* One night he was cleaning the attic and found his father's old suitcase. Inside was a wasp nest. The cosmonaut boy had traded it to the sanitation worker's son for some comic books, convincing him and the other baseball boys these were the same wasps from *The Monster from Green Hell* and their sting was an aphrodisiac that would make them irresistible to the cheerleaders. The sanitation worker woke up his son and they hauled the suitcase down to the gutter before plugging the glory holes carved on each side and dousing it in gasoline. They compared fingers blistered with stings. They listened to the crazed humming as the wasps burned and hissed in their own juices, speaking riddles in a secret alphabet.

Nobody was at school when the Russians launched Sputnik. He ran out of the classroom waving his fingers that seemed to say, The Russians are coming! The Russians are coming!

But it wasn't the Russians. It was a dust storm. The sky turned green, then black like a sad, crisp lung. When it was over the crops were all torn up. Cars piled on the highway. A sheep dangled from the telephone wire like a luckless trapeze artist.

The bishop found Nobody lying in the church pew as if he'd been licked by a dusty tongue. The boy had cut his hands breaking through the window trying to escape the storm. The hymnbook pages were all bloody.

Nobody's fingers moved slowly, flecking blood over the pews. Did you know obituary and orbit come from the same word? Obitus is what they used to call a visit to the low places. Like when the sun disappears into the horizon. Orbita is the trace left in the ground by a passing wheel. Like a scar on the earth. Obit. Orbit. Does that mean death is just another orbit? his fingers seemed to wonder.

I can't understand a word you're saying, the bishop said. He was a fat man, like a cross between a Merovingian and an elegant hippopotamus. Nobody said he ate so much because he was scared God might take him at any moment, so he put his faith in the laws of gravity.

They walked through the highway pile-up. The school bus had flipped on its side. Hogs without heads roamed the wreckage of the livestock truck. A tongue of blood and oil slicked the asphalt. People wandered around caked in dust. A woman in a glittery dress hobbled around looking for the foot she'd lost. Bewilderness, Nobody's fingers seemed to say.

Nothing anybody can do, the bishop muttered.

Won't you help them? Nobody's fingers seemed to say.

There's only one way to Mormon, the bishop said as they kept walking. I've read the Book of Mormon four hundred and eighty-six times. It doesn't say anything about aliens in the last days, so either you're not what you think you are, or this is no apocalypse.

The sky was yellow haze. They kept walking.

You look like a retarded tree, the bishop said when Nobody scratched his elbows until they were bleeding. Bewilderness, Nobody's fingers seemed to say. The bishop said all the medicine in the world can't cure what a baptism will do.

I have a foot in two worlds, Nobody's fingers seemed to say.

What would your mother say if she knew you were unbaptized? the bishop said.

My mother never wanted me here, Nobody's fingers seemed to say.

It was her dream for you to join us at church, the bishop said.

Sometimes Li Bai comes to me in my dreams, Nobody's fingers seemed to say.

Did you know the prophet Brigham Young said an unbaptized soul can leave the body? the bishop said. That's why the world is full of sinners. If a soul goes too long without the right baptism it can float all the way to the moon. Imagine that.

Do you know Li Bai? Nobody's fingers seemed to ask. The poet of many names and many deaths. The poet of wine and sex. The poet of exile and excess. The poet of stillness. Do you know what happened to him?

Jesus, what happened to you? the bishop asked, tapping his finger against the bullet hole in Nobody's fishbowl helmet.

Nobody knows, the boy's fingers seemed to say.

Cross the Sea of Years

Hours before he was bludgeoned to death at his workbench, the watchmaker's mind took a strange bounce and spun like a foursquare ball as he suddenly remembered the bedtime stories his father told him about sealing off the uranium mine shaft after emptying thousands of gallons of saltwater down there hoping to slow down the radioactive decay. When he climaxed with the prostitute, his fourth this week, the watchmaker closed his eyes and saw biohazard cannisters full of pitchblende floating under the town in circular, subterranean caverns, like weird castaways from a shipwreck. He knew it was only a matter of time. He owned more than a thousand timepieces but never wore his watch unless making love: a Waltham his father had worn in the Pacific theatre, and his father before him in the trenches at Verdun, silver-plated with a round face and seventeen jewel movement that fit snugly on the wrist. Once his escorts fell asleep, he would sneak downstairs to the workshop beneath the loft and adjust the time by two or three milliseconds to sync with the atomic clock in Albuquerque. It was a difficult time for timekeepers. No more pocket watch repairs, no more house calls for the grandfather clocks—it was all batteries and digital wristwatches with neon bands. He felt the clock inside him slowly ticking, the clock inside him that said everything is different but nothing is changing, because nature is a magician and change is her illusion, the clock inside him that said time is a cosmonaut swimming through a black hole, many moments splintering into and away from one another randomly, like inside a kaleidoscope, reminding him that there is a design and a designer, but we're all just eternal tadpoles to him, stuck in the swamp dreaming of an invisible frog in the sky, just matter plus magic plus time. The watchmaker stayed put, watching the watches, staring past the arroyo that stretched like a long hot scar, measuring the days by the flock of satellites passing in front of the full moon, there, like black crumbs falling off God's messy dinner plate. Three. Two. One.

Down the K-Hole

The dentist waited in the supermarket checkout line, zipping and unzipping his fanny pack, then biting his nails until they bled, assuring the cosmonaut boy tapping fingers on his watch that the mothership wasn't going anywhere, and once they cashed the foster parent check the dentist suggested they get clean, that it would only take a few days, but instead they spent half the money at the arcade before doing a bump of Special K in the bathroom stall, and during the whack-a-mole game the dentist asked the boy if he had ever had a wet dick, because that's the only baptism he really needed and he said, Let's go have another bump, but the cosmonaut boy didn't want to lose his place in line for the Skee-Ball, ignoring the dentist who said he didn't want to do it alone because Special K feels like watersliding down God's intestines and being shit out into stars, after which they argued whether He-Man could beat Hulk Hogan in a wrestling match before finding themselves at the funeral for the opera singer, so they hid in the empty baptismal font where someone had scratched on the tile LIFE IS AN IMMENSE DREAM, and the dentist said maybe the boy should get baptized and have all his sins wiped clean because it's just water, he didn't have to believe it, it's just words, and the cosmonaut boy's fingers seemed to say, Why's it so hard to believe what I am? and the dentist said he'd fit right in with the rest of them, because the Mormons had crazy beliefs too and loved outer space, believing this world is just a gas station along the highway of eternal life, and we lived for millions of years before being born and we'll live for millions of years after it because to be a Mormon is to be an alien castaway, he said, and neither of them had ever met the opera singer who was first diagnosed with cancer forty years ago and welcomed help from the sisters in the Relief Society after she lost all her hair, the sisters insisting this was not the kind of town to let a talented woman go bald and rallied together to find her a wig, but seeing as the synthetic wigs from France were too expensive, and the local goat, beaver, horse, and bear varieties did not do justice to the opera singer's talent and beauty, the sisters—after much prayer—determined they would shave their pubic zones, something their husbands had been trying to persuade them to do for some time, and donate what they could to make a wig, each according to her ability, the sisters said, and somehow the opera singer made a miraculous recovery and, believing it was a good luck charm, had hardly taken off the wig in four decades, but viewing the corpse the dentist whispered to the cosmonaut boy that he'd changed his mind, that maybe he shouldn't get baptized because once you take the drink there's no getting clean from it and the cosmonaut boy's fingers seemed to say, Tommy Lasorda looks like circumcised foreskin that evolved, and walking home the dentist said, You're worse than any drug, you're like gasoline in my veins, the dentist said, and the cosmonaut boy crawled through the window head over heels, and when the dentist leaned over the windowsill the boy wasn't there, even after he checked the closets and under the bed, even inside the fridge where the light bulb flickered and murmured, like it was the boy trying to tell him something, and the weeks passed and he couldn't sleep so he reported the boy missing but the police said it should be fine.

Along the Straits of Fear

It is with sadness we communicate the passing of the traveling salesman. Before his convalescence at the State Hospital with complications from gonorrhea, he enjoyed quite a bit of success in our town peddling various household items. Vacuum cleaners, pomade, perfumes, soaps. Most of these ended up in the landfill as yet another offering to our eternal optimism. One year, the salesman organized an exhibition in town hall to demonstrate his latest so-called revolutionary product. Unlatching a small vellum suitcase, he displayed a series of empty glass jars. One by one, volunteers were encouraged to open and inhale the contents. It's nothing but air, someone complained. Yes, the salesman said, from Tokyo. There was air from Montreal too. And Geneva. And Oslo. Cooler air, the salesman explained, was not just superior quality but a substantial bargain compared to humid, tropical air sold by inferior salesmen. The salesman then displayed a tiny glass vial. Celestial air, he smiled, the same air that God breathes. After sampling it, people walked around in a daze. He distributed brochures with illustrations detailing the harvesting of air in large nets before it was sealed in the vials just like the ones in his suitcase. The samples sold quickly. Police were summoned to quiet the unruly crowd. Within a matter of days, the city was in a panic. Children gasped for air in doorways and fathers sprawled out in gutters. Patients overwhelmed the hospital, insisting they had used up their air supply and were unable to breathe. At least eleven people died of so-called asphyxiation. One of the psychiatrists who works

at the State Hospital says that before passing, the salesman
was quite insane. His gums were mushy beets, the few
teeth he had left wobbling like stained dominos. I got to
get out of this place, he said, can't you feel it? This world
trying to touch another? He often held his breath for long
periods of time hoping to avoid infection. Not the pesticides or chemtrails that were unavoidable in this desert,
he said, but the fantasies that are like air, traveling breath
to breath in search of a body to possess.

Let Me Take You There

On Wednesday evenings, the school principal's son drove himself to the Mormon youth group where he continued his education on the Satanic power of coffee, the three handshakes needed to discern angelic messengers, and how to avoid heavy petting before marriage. He sewed his own pioneer costume for the Mountain Meadows pageant reenactment and pulled a handcart through the DI parking lot. He wrote the lyrics for a musical skit about baptizing the dead spirits lost to AIDS. You were one of God's generals in heaven before this world, the bishop told him. He dreamt of a man in a suit with lambchop sideburns feeding him a golden potato. He woke up with a stomach ache. His mother said it meant he shouldn't drive the car. His father said the hairy man from his dream was probably Bigfoot, the child of Cain, and it meant they should buy more food storage before the next stock market crash. The boy died in a car accident later that night. Drove right off the bridge into the creek by a drunk in a golden Cadillac. His little brother, who was sleeping in the back seat and miraculously survived with only cuts and bruises, was catatonic for weeks. In Sunday school he scratched anarchy symbols on his arm. Instead of playing baseball with the other boys he watched old 50s sci-fi movies about radioactive brains from outer space terrorizing cities in metallic womb containers and floating like possessed balloons hypnotizing foxy lab assistants. When he turned twelve the Mormons gave him their priesthood and, believing he was like Moses in Egypt, he swapped all the dead frogs for biology dissection with live ones and pretended to resurrect them with a prayer. His parents took him to a shrink who started him on Adderall. It stopped his heart twice, but the paramedics saved him. When he returned to school, he drooled a little and one eye twitched. At recess, he went under the bleachers with a girl who wanted to see the scars from the accident. Is it true you died and came back? she wondered. He shrugged and tried to unfasten her bra. When she asked what he was doing he said he was a general in heaven and could do whatever he wanted.

Scabs

It was the winter half the middle-school teachers got laid off for doctoring test scores. The principal resigned. Then the bus drivers went on strike and the cafeteria staff started sharing their pantry vodka with any student who knew the secret password. The substitute English teacher, who also taught wood shop, was lousy. He had everyone memorize Latin roots and diagram their sentences which were then cut onto wood blocks. During silent reading periods he paced the room, the dog tags tinkling under his shirt. His arms were hairy. He rode all over town on a white horse. He wore Birkenstocks. He didn't cut his hair and said no bullet or knife could hurt him. His breath smelled of sauerkraut. His critiques were savage. *Your penmanship makes me wish I was in the gulag* and *This diorama doesn't feel authentic.* Thundercats *is for pussies,* he told the kids passing notes, *it's like you've never heard of* Gravity's Rainbow. He read the students a poem he'd written about drinking kombucha with Brigham Young's ghost inside the Disneyland Haunted Mansion. He kept the cosmonaut boy in detention and listened to his fingers that seemed to say, Baseball is for freaks. The spitballers, the crackerjackers, the sign stealers, the balkers, the juicers, the knucklers, the southpaws, the suicide squeezers, the submariners, the chin music, the bat kissing, the pine tar-ring, the pickling, the unwashed jock straps, the curses. Look at this ball with all these stitches, his fingers seemed to say, like a little Frankenstein. During recess the substitute clipped his waxy, yellowed toenails that looked like dinosaur scales. He let them grow until they curled over the tips of his toes. He brought in projector slides of a trip to Peru and talked about how as the glaciers melted ten thousand years ago the giant sloth was not like the reindeer that migrated north with the ice but was hunted into extinction. Other sloths saved themselves by evolving smaller and smaller and going blind, fleeing to the trees where they used long nails to hang upside-down, moving slower and slower to try and cheat death. Not long after new teachers were hired, the substitute hanged himself. He left nothing behind except an extensive toenail collection. They were arranged in glass vials of uniform shape about the size of spice containers. Each vial was labeled by year going back a decade. They filled kitchen cupboards and closets. A lawyer went door-to-door distributing the toenails to school children per the wishes of the substitute's last will and testament. They rested on windowsills where in the evening the sun cracked its runny egg yolk over the horizon, the light twisting through the maze of jarred toenails and refracting across the floor like a weird, beautiful kaleidoscope.

Olly Olly Oxen Free

It is with sadness we communicate the passing of our Baba who never married and only ever wore black. Her right arm was longer than the left. From too much hugging, she joked. The children hated her. They said she had zippers on her forehead. We laughed and said those were just wrinkles. For a small fee she'd show up at your house and pretend to be your Baba. A rent-a-grandmother. She baked cookies and played teatime. She taught the children hide-and-go-seek. She sang lullabies and showed children her collection of Vaseline glass. She bought them at flea markets all over the state. Plates, teacups, silverware, decanters, and candlesticks all laced with uranium. At night they glowed pale neon green. When she visited, she gave the children a piece of glass to keep by their bed. A nightbright, she called them. The cosmonaut boy got a necklace. His fingers trembled over the beads as the dentist flicked the syringe and pulled the boy's foot closer. He pulled it back. Do you want to stop? the dentist said, and the space helmet sort of nodded, sort of shook gently. The dentist promised it was just one more bump and then the voices would stop. Just one more bump and then he promised he would teach him how to play baseball: how to throw a ball, how to swing a bat, how to grab his dick and spit. What's it feel like in there? the dentist said, tapping his finger against the helmet, is it any better than what it feels like out here? Why do you stay? the cosmonaut boy's dreamy fingers seemed to say, and the dentist said, I don't even know your name. You dumb boy, our Baba laughed as she packed up her radioactive trinkets and put on her coat, Nobody knows his name. Yeah, well, nobody asked you, the dentist said. You're a witch, the cosmonaut boy's fingers seemed to say. I'm like you, our Baba said, tracing her finger in the boy's hand. Sometimes I feel like I'm in a game of pickle, the cosmonaut boy's fingers seemed to say, just circling the bases. Take my hand, our Baba said, and you can be one of my children. The cosmonaut boy's sticky milkshake fingers pointed at the sky. Don't listen to her, the dentist said, his voice slow and scratchy, don't go all saintsick. It's too late, the cosmonaut boy's fingers seemed to say as he stumbled out the door to play with the other children. Their hair had turned white, their skins pale. The church elders had tried to stop it from getting worse by calling down blessings from heaven and baptizing all the kids again, but nothing worked. It's the nightbrights, our Baba said. Her spit was white like angel tears and her teeth rattled like loose piano keys. More and more children had white hair and pale skins. The games of hide-and-go-seek lasted longer. The sun went down. Nobody could be found.

Nobody was allowed in the church. Nobody's clean enough to come inside, the bishop told the injured spread out on the grass outside the chapel after the highway pile-up, you'll just make a mess. The dust storm moved west. Babies cried. A man stuffed gauze into his father's stomach wound. When he ran out of gauze, he filled it with corn husks, but it didn't stop the bleeding.

We're going to need more corn, the man said.

I'm not a scarecrow, the father said.

Nobody wore a white jumpsuit. The bishop stitched the cuts on his hands. Feel anything? he asked. Nobody didn't answer. He looked at the sky filled with clouds like sick livers. He moved his fingers and the wounds opened up again.

Whatever you're saying, the bishop said as he started over with the stitches, I don't believe it.

You don't know what you're doing, his fingers seemed to say.

What's that supposed to be? the bishop said, his twitchy fingers mocking the boy, it's all Japanese to me. Stop pretending like you're some alien.

Nobody taught me how to be quiet, Nobody's fingers seemed to say.

You know your soul is in trouble, the bishop said.

Nobody has a soul, his fingers seemed to say.

Did I ever tell you I was almost Butch Cassidy? the bishop said, his face sort of twisted as if digging a splinter from under his nail. We were boys breaking wild horses in Frisco. He went his way, and I went mine, the bishop said. Life is funny like that. Nobody has any idea what God will turn you into.

I don't want to be here anymore, Nobody's fingers seemed to say.

It's a privilege to be characters in His movie, the bishop said.

What's the sign for privilege? Nobody extended his middle finger. The skin opened again and started bleeding. The bishop kept stitching.

A young girl shuffled in circles near the window. She wore a torn, dusty dress. The road rash stretched from her neck to her knees with skin dangling off her like Christmas tinsel. The bishop said she would be dead in five minutes. She kept asking for someone to dance with her. She said she couldn't believe she wasn't married yet.

It's like someone's having a bad dream inside my teeth, Nobody's fingers seemed to say.

Say a prayer and this will all be over, the bishop said.

Oh, you wayfarers from afar, Nobody's fingers seemed to say, reciting the poems of Li Bai, why do you come hither on this direful road?

We were warned, the bishop said, God warned us he would give us this desert as a land of milk and honey but if we hearkened unto the voice of strangers and aliens in the land, then the Lord shall make a rain of powder and dust and smite thee with the scab and with the itch whereof thou canst be healed.

Oh, why go you west, I pray? *Nobody's fingers seemed to say.*

Only you can pray it away, the bishop said.

And when will you return? *Nobody's fingers seemed to say*

It's there, the bishop said. The power is in your mouth. Pray it. I fear for you.

Go on, boy, pray it. Pray it.

Sit with Elders of a Gentle Race

A woman from the superintendent's office visited the classroom to administer an aptitude test. She called herself the Colonel even though she had never enlisted, much less fought in a war, or even fired a weapon. The children were excited and nervous to learn about their futures. Mechanic, nurse, astronaut, banker. But really alcoholic, prostitute, runaway, cocaine junkie. Of course, the Colonel was only there on behalf of the military trying to recruit the morally flexible who wouldn't have nightmares about anonymously dropping bombs on remote villages. The cosmonaut boy, dreaming he would be recruited into military aerospace, qualified as a landscaper. There's no grass on Planet X, his fingers seemed to say, everything is ice, and the dentist shrugged and told him at least it didn't say he was human. He huffed the yellowed pocket square and said these were the only things that made him feel normal. They watched *X the Unknown*. Let's go to church, the dentist said, and they put on suits and sneakers, but instead crawled through a broken window of the dentist's old middle school that was being bulldozed. Snow fell through a hole in the roof. The dentist told the cosmonaut boy how his father used to take him to play in the snow even though he hated it. His father loved God but couldn't understand why he made beautiful things so fragile. He was a hard man. He told the dentist he wasn't allowed to play baseball because it was a game of deceit, but the dentist knew it was because his father was a nobody and wanted his son to be just like him. He never had a useful thought, the dentist said. He never drank a bottle of wine slowly at sunrise, or danced quietly in the rain before making love, never smelled the wildflowers at sunset, or closed his eyes and took long curious maniacal breaths until his lungs burned. He never knew how to be slow. He was in such a hurry to be dead that his only pleasure was in dying slowly his whole life. But I'm not my old man, the dentist said, my life is just— and then he paused for a long while and stared down the dark middle school hallway with a collapsed ceiling leaking water. Inside one of the classrooms they found the Colonel. She was naked. One eye was swollen and purple and the dark blood coming from the bullet hole on the side of her face had dried, but otherwise she didn't look dead. The note in her hand said, *Grief is a drug.* The cosmonaut boy put his finger in the bullet hole. She was still warm and oily. It was like all the dark in the room was coming from where her legs butterflied. The cosmonaut boy leaned closer. What kind of mad God, his fingers seemed to say, has us crawl out a bearded hot dog bun turned sideways to dance in circus cages? They walked back into the street. Jesus, I wish we hadn't seen that, the dentist said. He burned the Colonel's suicide note with a match. We'll tell someone, the dentist said. They watched the falling snow. They didn't move. Can you really not hear us, the dentist said, or are you just pretending? The cosmonaut boy's fingers seemed to say, Yes.

Deceased Alive

It is with sadness we communicate the passing of the buffet meat carver who was found dead in the trailer park. He manned the roast beef carving station every night at the Chuck-A-Rama looking somewhat comical but majestic in his heavy apron and toque blanche. There was a certain fungal charm about the man as he sharpened his knife before every cut—not too thick and not too thin, the goldilocks of butchers—and encouraged patrons to eat as much as they could. This is the last great age of addiction, the meat carver told us, and whether it's love busyness sex brains money or freedom, everyone's an addict, everyone's a dealer, the meat carver philosophized. It was only after he died that anyone learned he checked out *Playboys* from the library, cutting out the nude heads and replacing them with portraits of Nancy Reagan, and volunteered at the nursing home reading from his yellowed copy of *Atlas Shrugged*. Around the same time the buffet carver was gassing himself with carbon monoxide, the cosmonaut boy—who was one of the last patrons to see the deceased alive—swept broken glass off the floor before pulling the rag away from the dentist's swollen cheek. One side of his face, from lips to his ear, had been sliced open like a birthday cake. He held the mirror while the dentist finished his own stitches and applied gauze soaked in whiskey, assuring him that two smiles are better than one but next time don't try and cheat the blue lady, because even the cosmonaut boy knew it was unwise to tango with that woman after he spiked the sacrament water with laxatives and she shit herself at the pulpit mid-prayer. Don't listen to her, she's not a nice person, the dentist said sewing his face back together, she'll only tell you what you want to hear. I'm hungry for love, the cosmonaut boy's fingers seemed to say. She's not the gentle crackpot everyone thinks she is, the dentist said. I always thought love was something you ate until you got full, the cosmonaut boy's fingers seemed to say, and then you ate more of it until you're sick. We're the same, you and me, the dentist said after he had a whippit. But I think maybe love is more of a baby growing inside you, the cosmonaut boy's fingers seemed to say, a little monster you carry around until you don't feel like yourself anymore, until you're not the same clucking person you used to be. Why are you doing this? the dentist said, fixing a bump of Special K for the cosmonaut boy. And then you put baby Lovenstein on someone's doorstep without them knowing, the cosmonaut boy's fingers seemed to say, but why would you do this? The dentist winced as his second smile unstitched and said, Nobody else is. Do you think that's how they love on Planet X, the cosmonaut boy's fingers seemed to say, is love a monster-gifting party? Do me a favor, the dentist said, when you get back to Planet X, don't tell them about this place. Just pretend this never happened. Otherwise they'll make you remember everything. The temples, the crickets, the magic underwear. They'll turn it into scripture. They'll make you a prophet. They'll worship what you say. And you'll love it. You'll love believing in your own words. It's like having a whippit only it kills you. Then the cosmonaut boy curled inside the neighbor's satellite dish as the dentist hijacked the signal, scrambling the first news footage of the frothy green clouds over the shantytowns of Bhopal bringing everyone to their knees.

Blood Blisters

They weren't real sisters. They met at the funeral of an old lady when they were little girls. While everyone sang hymns, they took turns on the tire swing outside the chapel. Blood blisters, they clasped hands and promised each other. They dressed in twin costumes that Halloween as inmates escaped from the State Hospital for Melancholics and Other Incurables. Meal sack dresses with white bonnets and leathery chicken feet they gathered from the slaughterhouse skinned and stretched and pressed and stitched into masks. Stray dogs followed them house to house. The slightly taller one got a job the next summer at the Ouroboros Theatre in the ticket booth, followed by the slightly shorter one who got the same job the next month. They worked their way to the concession stand, then ushers, and finally projectionists where they got to watch all the new movies the night before anyone else. After the theatre burned down, they pooled their money to renovate it and screened old campy sci-fi films. Black and white ones only, because color ruined everything. The blood blisters loved the cosmonaut boy. They gave him free popcorn and even shared their secret way to tell them apart: one of them liked to cut herself on the thighs, leaving behind long milky scars. A skin alphabet, she called it. She couldn't help herself. It was a compulsion, a kind of worship. The cosmonaut boy showed them the scaly pink patches on his knees and elbows, like a swirl of human and alien alphabets that reminded him of the time he was blown-up and had to be stitched back together again.

That was his secret: I am a traveler of both time and space. He was invited to the wedding of one of the blood blisters. It happened inside the theatre lobby. Before signing her name on the certificate, the bride escaped through the back doors and, successfully outrunning her fiancé, threw herself off the bridge. To prove, her blood blister later said, she was still sane.

Nobody got polio. He was climbing the jungle gym when it came for him. He fell with a slow woosh. The sound of his helmet hitting the sand was like when an axe goes into a piece of rotted wood, the only sound we'd ever heard him make. We thought it was a trick. All those years teasing him and now Nobody was fooling us. Even when they put him in the iron lung, we thought he was faking it.

Bedridden inside the machine, he lay perfectly still. His fishbowl head stuck out at one end. The nurse fixed a mirror so he could see his reflection. Even after the doctors said he could leave he just lay there.

We told Nobody he wasn't sick anymore. We told him he could go back to filling the school toilets with a thousand white salamanders and using the Bunsen burners in chem lab for blue darts and threatening to stick a cube of butter up the principal's butt. But Nobody didn't want to leave the iron lung. He was tired of living in a fridge at the bottom of a landfill like the aliens from Invasion of the Saucer Men. *He was tired of being the fiend without a face. He was tired of tuning the ham radio every night for the mothership that never came. Nobody said he was tired of time traveling every time he walked through a door. Always this desert, always this life, always the same kinds of people, it never ended, just hiccupping through time. Nobody wanted to be still.*

The bishop sat with Nobody at the hospital. He fed pieces of sacrament bread down the oxygen hose, not paying attention to Nobody's fingers remembering how after the meteor crashed in the desert he'd baked the sacrament bread using his own shit, telling everyone only his alien fluids could protect the congregation from the beast with a million eyes, but nobody believed him, so he stood at the pulpit in the suit two sizes too big and ate it himself, the entire loaf, until he threw it up.

It's monstrous what they did to you, the bishop said, tracing a finger over the space helmet.

Maybe I put this on myself, Nobody's fingers seemed to say, maybe there's a reason nobody can take it off.

But God works in mysterious ways, the bishop said, it's like he wants us to be alone so other people will find us.

Nobody's fingers seemed to say he was never alone. His brain was a haunted screen.

Sometimes I envy you, the bishop said. His voice was soft and surprisingly tender. So many useless sounds you don't have to hear.

Nobody's fingers seemed to say, Sometimes I bang my head against the wall trying to remember the sounds of home.

The bishop scratched the cracks in the glass with a finger. It's awful, isn't it, the silence?

And when your head doesn't hurt the silence is beautiful, Nobody's fingers seemed to say, you can imagine anything when it's quiet.

The bishop said, If you don't feel sound do you even exist?

Faithsick

It is with sadness we communicate the passing of the trapeze artist who died yesterday in an accident involving the cosmonaut boy's catapult. He discovered his trade late in life. Love at first sight, he said. Maybe the desire for ecstasy and foolishness started when he was a boy. The way his father threw him up in the air and caught him every time. Higher, higher, never tiring, always pulling him close at the end of his little flights. Until he stopped catching him, stopped hugging him, stopped looking at him even, betrayed by the little man who had replaced his boy. But the trapeze artist couldn't stop thinking about that feeling of suspension. It was a stupid human trick. But something else too. A kind of faith. It frightened him. What was there to do up there? Sometimes the trapeze artist glanced around. Other times he waved. Was it hello or goodbye? Even he wasn't sure. It frightened him more. But he kept chasing that feeling. Like any artist, he died several times before his actual death yesterday. But he kept trapezing anyway. He'd tried many times to do a somersault on the ground but found it impossible. Only in the air could he manage such an absurd horror as going head over heels. There was nothing free about it. On the contrary. Swinging, flying, floating, upside-down. He was addicted to gravity. The invisible tugging of the universe that made possible the moment between floating and falling. The purgatory, he called it, where the body dances at the edge of the abyss. This fearsome wonderful maddening sickening affectionate alien nowhereness. It's there

at your fingertips, the trapeze artist used to say, lasting for
an instant, and then is gone.

This World Has Seldom Seen

This is the last known photograph of the blind man. Some boys scavenging for arrowheads found him at the bottom of the ravine yesterday, his white beard yellowed by bad weather. He looked like God, they said. A note in his pocket indicated no tears should be wept for him and that he died believing this was the best of all possible worlds. He is survived by the cactus, his one true love. Nobody had ever seen a Saguaro grow north of Arizona. The blind man discovered the cactus as a boy. Love at first touch, he said. All his friends were interested in nudie magazines or lying about their age to enlist, but the blind man took long walks into the desert to feel the cactus needles against his fingertips and bring it buckets of water. Sometimes he gave it shade with a little umbrella. Mostly he talked to it. Nobody knows what. But when the mayor tried to have the cactus removed for the new highway, the blind man went straight to the courthouse. He's gone too far, half the town said, calling the marriage of a man and a cactus obscene. The other half said it was beautiful. Most just wanted to see proof of consummation. You know it's a myth these things are full of water, the dentist told the cosmonaut boy whose finger pricked the cactus spines. They sat in the shade. We should go to church, the dentist said. I'm thirsty, the cosmonaut boy's fingers seemed to say. The dentist took a handful of pills. She got me hooked, he said, people forget that. Every little town like this needs a demon and a saint. Maybe we were happy. I don't remember. The cosmonaut boy broke off one of the cactus arms. It oozed sap.

Everything out here is just full of ghosts, his fingers seemed to say. She used to say she knew where I hid the zipper to my skin, the dentist said, and she would crawl inside me and I knew where to find hers. We spent years like that. Two unzipped fools laying on a bed of dust. I don't see how you people breathe this stuff, the cosmonaut boy's fingers seemed to say as a handful of dust slipped between his fingers, it's like you're born to choke on the thing you're made of. I had no idea you can drown in the desert, the dentist said, nobody ever does. It was only a few weeks ago another Saguaro started growing not far from the blind man's cactus. He was distraught. Who could blame him for cutting it down? It was love. Strange, forbidden, no doubt perverse, but the great romance of our town. He was last seen at the canyon's edge overlooking the ravine where he liked to listen to the horizon. Nobody in town enjoys this sight more than me, the blind man always said. He was seventy-two.

It is with sadness we communicate the passing of the computer programmer, an amateur bird watcher who was religiously devoted to his computer, the Synchro Unifying Sinometric Integrating Equitensor, or SUSIE, an artificially intelligent system which, the programmer believed, would soon be the cure for loneliness. As a boy, his only friends were birds, spying them from his windows ever since hearing about the firebird, an old Russian story his mother read to him with a glass of warm milk and cookies. His father said bird watching was for commie fags and would never put food on the table. The computer programmer tried to convince the local birdwatching group—the twitchers, they called themselves—to listen to SUSIE speak the language of birds. They wore matching windbreakers and sneakers and sat in the café drinking fruity teas and talking about warblers and waxwings and juncos. The computer programmer got the courage one morning to ask if any of them had seen a wild sapsucker, a nocturnal variety of woodpecker with a ruby throat that wraps its tongue around its brain to prevent injury while pecking trees. His own tongue, he told the twitchers, seemed fairly useless by comparison. He told them how he'd spent years listening to one after it nested in a utility pole outside his window, transcribing its nightly songs into algorithms and feeding them to SUSIE because the music helped him forget his life. Almost kissed a girl in high school. Almost drafted for the war. That time he almost won the lottery. His mother who almost avoided cancer. Almost joined the circus as a unicyclist. Almost a genius, but either SUSIE's translations said *Error* or gibberish things like, *The heart is a windswept vein*, and her only real use was playing back staticky synth-pop versions of sapsucker songs. What the computer programmer couldn't understand was whether SUSIE meant vein, or vane, or vain, and when the twitchers ignored him he told the cosmonaut boy he felt like he was going insane, like he was this close to blowing his brains out once and for all, and the cosmonaut boy's fingers seemed to say that this place has all the uselessness of a dream and that makes it so hard to quit. In the nature of things, the computer programmer's obsession proved too much and, after trapping the sapsucker, kept it in a dark cage and gorged it for weeks on grapes and figs before drowning it in cognac. He then plucked it and roasted it whole—legs and all—in a cassoulet with salt and pepper until golden brown, and the bones had turned to gelatin. Placing the entire bird in his mouth, he covered his face with a napkin so God wouldn't see and bit down. The hot syrup of tissues and organs swam in his mouth as the ambrosial fat cascaded down his throat. It was like I could taste the bird's entire life, he told the cosmonaut boy. Late last night, after the storm, the computer programmer found three broken sapsucker eggs in the gutter. A fourth was still intact. He climbed the utility pole. Near the nest he lost his footing and, in a panic, grabbed one of the wires. The twitchers, perched in neighboring trees listening to SUSIE's electronic songs, said there was a flash of light and the computer programmer made a sound almost like a bird. His shadow flapped wildly, tumbling into bare sky.

Leave the Path that Led Me to That Place

Just as the train roared into the stockyards last night, a worker stumbled too close to the platform's edge and was smartly bisected by the incoming locomotive. Half the man fell onto the rails while the other half remained on the platform. It was a gruesome scene. His wife arrived in time to share a private moment with the bisected man on the rails who lovingly touched his wife's lips and curled a finger in her hair. The other half, twisted on the platform, muttered obscenities while the crowd watched. When asked if she wished to say anything to her husband's other half the woman refused, confessing her husband was a drunk and often violently beat her. This, she said, pulling her half husband closer to her, is the man I've been waiting to fall back in love with all my life.

Yellow Desert Scream

The first time the cheerleader died was playing Atari. There was an advertisement at the shopping mall for a video game giveaway, but it was only after she got there she realized it was a scam. The bishop was handing out Books of Mormon and threatening to baptize kids who never went to church. Out by the dumpsters, the cheerleader found a crumpled twenty-dollar bill. She gave the store clerk a blowjob to cover the rest of the console cost. She broke up with her boyfriend. She quit cheerleading. She subscribed to magazines like *Atari Age* and *Game Brain* under the alias Q*Bitch. Her days were spent with *Ms. Pac-Man*, *Frogger*, and *Pitfall!* Her favorite was Q*Bert. A weird but cute alien that hopped diagonally up and down a pyramid and swore incoherently whenever a purple snake bit him. Every level was a new puzzle, which felt no different to the cheerleader than middle school. During a marathon that lasted eighty-nine hours and fifty-six minutes she scored 37,163,081 points. She snapped a Polaroid to send to Guiness World Records. Then her heart stopped. The second time the cheerleader died was during a field trip to the traveling science museum. While everyone else looked at jellyfish and slices of Albert Einstein's brain that looked like bologna, she studied the Chernobyl babies exhibit. They were floating in jars with pickled, lopsided faces. Their eyes were sewn shut. The cheerleader couldn't tell if that was for their sake or hers. She tried not to think about it. One of the teachers vomited but the cheerleader stood there mesmerized. That's when one of the Chernobyl babies winked at her. The museum curator said that was impossible. But the cheerleader knew. Later that night she dreamt she was Gorbachev's barber. She trimmed the grey hairs around his ears and polished the top of his head with a radioactive sponge until his scalp was shiny and the birthmark rubbed away. Then she wrung the sponge into sacrament cups. It looked like wine. Everyone at church who drank it melted except for her. The cheerleader went back to the exhibit every day for a month, dropping dead yesterday of exhaustion, but as far as anyone knows the Chernobyl babies never winked for her again.

Blind Stitch

The house at the end of the road, designed by the architect who went mad and hanged himself in the attic, looked like two houses nested inside one another. A roof grew out of the porch and there were doors where there should have been chimneys. Inside, the rooms, hallways, and stairwells blurred together, overlapping like a mouth trying to swallow itself. The old man who lived there was something of a paraplegic. He spent all day on the porch in his wheelchair. His face was wrinkled and he looked unhinged from time. His only visitor was the dentist. He came on Sundays with a bag of bread and a bottle of sparkling water. He pretended to bless it and told the old paraplegic it was sacrament. The old man chewed slowly. He sipped the water carefully. He liked the bubbles in his throat. The dentist lied and told the old paraplegic he was looking better and should recover soon, that any day now he'd be walking on his own and don't be surprised if he didn't come next week, but the dentist always came every Sunday and said the same thing. Sometimes the cosmonaut boy came with him and held the green Tupperware bowl to collect the old man's bloody spit while the dentist cleaned his rotted teeth. It used to be this place was quiet, the dentist said. A tree, a tire swing, a little wind. That was enough. It was a real desert back then. Now it's just noise. The radios, the televisions, the electric hum of wires. Sometimes I wake up in the middle of the night and can hear the plutonium in the silos underground, little radioactive babies crying in their warhead cradles. So much sound like a dream you can't wake up from. You don't know how lucky you are, the dentist said, tapping a finger on the boy's space helmet. For someone who loves quiet you never shut the hell up, the paraplegic said. The dentist half-smiled and said, I forget what it's like talking with real people. You can't keep him here, you know, the paraplegic spat into the bowl, he doesn't belong here. The dentist said, I'm the only home he's got. His home is out there, the paraplegic said, waving a hand at the desert, let God sort him out. The dentist said, I used to think like you, praying that God would tie up all the loose ends, but look at that sky. Light and empty space. The world grinds us down to atoms, old man, and you either end up a hot boiling star or soft stuff in the dark places. Nobody's lucky, the cosmonaut boy's fingers seemed to say. They should put the two of you in a hospital, the paraplegic said, fools trying to talk like prophets. For good luck I'm wearing the same jock strap until I get back to the mothership, the cosmonaut boy's fingers seemed to say. The dentist wrapped the old man's gnarled feet in warm compresses, but the pain was too much so he gave him an injection. The paraplegic told the cosmonaut boy stories about how he used to be a ballerina at the finest opera house in Vienna. That was before his wife left and his son stopped coming to see him. I was a good person, the paraplegic said, a bad father and a bad husband, but a good person. He didn't remember their faces now. Your friend here is no friend, the paraplegic told the cosmonaut boy. Nothing goes to dust, you see? Nothing is still, nothing stays quiet. It's all a blur. That's the secret, said the paraplegic who a few hours later would throw himself off the balcony, never stop dancing in your

head, never stop spinning, never slow down, if you don't
breathe then the life can't get out.

The Spirit Line

It is with sadness we communicate the passing of the ex-marine who owned two suits, both black, which he wore on alternating days. He never married. He didn't own a telephone and ate one meal per day. Other than a desk his father carpentered during his troubled years and a Navajo rug, the house was empty. The rug hung on the parlor wall. Indians from the reservation had traded it for a chipped teacup the ex-marine pocketed from the rubble at Nagasaki. Once a month he pulled the rug off the nails for deep cleaning. He beat it free of dust before brushing out the fleas and beetles no bigger than a pinhead. He sprayed it with vinegar and gently scrubbed it with lemon rind. He spent hours admiring the design. The shapes were simple and geometrical with bright vegetal colors but dizzying as any labyrinth. The mirrored patterns appeared as different things on different days. Flying saucers, funnel clouds, a snake devouring itself, a woman's clitoris. The Indians told him that a weaver will twine part of her spirit into a rug but always hide a single flawed stitch, almost invisible to the naked eye, so as not to upset the gods. Sometimes these were stitches along the border where the weaver's soul could escape. Over the years, the ex-marine had convinced himself if he could find that small deliberate mistake among the thousands of other stitches, maybe his spirit and the weaver's could be together. His body, gently decomposed, was found yesterday. Apoplectic love.

Nobody wants to be normal anymore, the bishop said as he paced the hospital room, everyone wants a tortured soul. He sat next to the iron lung all night, tapping on the boy's helmet and asking, Are you still in there?

It's like a boundless dream in here, Nobody's fingers seemed to say, nothing and nobody to trouble us.

The bishop told Nobody to take off his helmet and have a little faith. You know you're not an alien, right?

Nobody's fingers seemed to say, I'm faithsick. It's a magnetic monster.

The bishop said all his life he'd been told he was destined for spiritual greatness. He said they promised him he would dream dreams and feel the voice of God burning in his ear. But the only spiritual experience he'd ever had was when he walked out into the desert and saw the old potash pond on fire and a naked woman swimming in it whose skin glittered like diamonds, but coming close to her he could see it wasn't skin at all but thousands of lips and they were moving without words, without sounds. Every Sunday he went to church wondering if this vision was from God or the devil. He told nobody. He said, Sometimes I think God made us bruised and broken so we'd go crawling back to him like beggars, like he's addicted to our love and wants us addicted to faith.

Nobody's fingers seemed to say, Maybe not everything is ours.

The bishop turned off the iron lung. The machine wheezed long and slow and then was quiet. I'm not a monster, he said.

Nobody's fingers seemed to say, You should see the future.

The bishop said, Even if I am, God will come and wipe away the tears for some and bring them for others.

Nobody's fingers seemed to say, Nothing happens the way

you imagine. The world just passes from us.

We're nobodies, the bishop said, just characters in His movie.

Do you think they play baseball on Planet X? Nobody's fingers seemed to say.

Let me tell you what keeps me up at night, the bishop said.

Real baseball, not the bush league nonsense in Los Angeles. Fuck the Dodgers, Nobody's fingers seemed to say. Fuck Koufax and Drysdale and Robinson and Lasorda. A bunch of pussies running away from Brooklyn. Give me the Say Hey Kid. Give me the Dominican Dandy, Stretch, the Baby Bull, and the Ancient Mariner. Give me real men with nicknames.

It's boys like you who don't want to be men, the bishop said, boys sitting around like a bunch of crickets thinking you're funny pitching voices to the wind and waiting to be eaten by gulls.

Do you know the saddest thing I've ever seen? Nobody's fingers seemed to say.

It's the saddest thing, the bishop said.

It was the Polo Grounds. Last game of the season, nineteen-thirty-something. Some nobody batting a buck-fifty was going to win the game for the Dodgers in extras, but before that, Nobody's fingers seemed to say, before the Giants lost the pennant, Master Mel rounded first to third in the greatest pickle in the history of baseball nobody remembers. You should have seen it. You had to be there to believe it.

The bishop traced his finger over the cracks in Nobody's helmet. What happened?

He didn't make it, Nobody's fingers seemed to say, he didn't make it home.

It was the bishop who helped Nobody out of the iron lung and convinced him the mothership would come tonight and he wouldn't be stuck human like the rest of us if he set fire to the

Ouroboros Theatre. Nobody danced with the flames and moved his fingers as if to say, I'm cured! as smoke and ash filled the sky.

When the fire trucks came, he leapt half-naked into the dumpster.

Nobody saw him again.

Dreaming the Wrong Catastrophe

The dentist found the cosmonaut boy with a dog leash around his neck tied to a lamppost in the church parking lot. Where have you been? the dentist said, I haven't seen you in months. I'm always here, the cosmonaut boy's fingers seemed to say. You can't just disappear like that, the dentist said. The boy picked at the scaly patches on his elbows, his fingers telling the dentist he'd gotten scared during the church Halloween party when the other kids took turns smashing a piñata that looked like him and that's when he peed himself. The baseball boys, who hated him ever since he baked the sacrament bread full of his shit that made the congregation sick, stretched the soggy underwear over his helmet and dragged him through the parking lot telling him to bark like a dog. Later, they sat in the post office. The dentist told the boy being a kid is bullshit. The cosmonaut boy's fingers seemed to say that ever since watching *I Married a Monster from Outer Space* he started to doubt he was an alien. This is Utah, the dentist said, there's no cure for it. The cosmonaut boy's fingers seemed to say the real disaster was the baseball boys burning down the catapult again. The dentist said there's no cure for people who see catastrophe as an aphrodisiac and believe in a God who's addicted to our shame. They stared at the post office marquee. Some drunk teenagers had scrambled the plastic letters so instead of reading Passport Appointments Only it now said Ass Ointments Lonely. The mailman was deaf in one ear. He was embarrassed by it, so he blamed it on his wife for talking to him in bed, and in the car, and at the dinner table every night. The same ear all these years. That wife voice. Wife-itis, he called it. And then she divorced him and airbrushed him out of the family photos, convincing everyone at church to pretend he was invisible. The cosmonaut boy filled out a passport application just in case he needed one to get on the mothership. He tried to give one to the dentist who shook his head. No thanks, I don't leave town anymore, he said, I have a condition. Haven't you heard? People say I'm sick, the dentist said, that I'm a junkie whose wife checked out. And they're right. I'm the sickest man I know. I can tell you about everyone in this town. I'm related to more than half of them. I know their secrets, I know their dreams, I know what they've lost going back five generations, and I know everything they've had in their mouths for forty-seven years, but I've never known any of them. We're strangers on a park bench tired and hot and sorry with friendliness. He huffed the pocket square. Do you have a word for that kind of sick on Planet X? Go on, have your fun, the mailman said, be like the rest of them and pretend like I'm not here, pretend like I don't see nobody, like I don't hear nobody. The mailman went home and, after eating a TV dinner, put his favorite Boy Scout pocketknife in his throat. The new mailman has two good ears and lets the kids lick all the stamps. Everybody loves the new mailman.

For Things Not Real

It is with sadness we communicate the passing of the chiropractor who died after a long and painful illness. He was fifty-five. He owned a dozen cars. He souped-up the engines and raced them on the salt flats with the other motorheads, sprawled afterwards on the hood like a pinup queen as he stared into the sun until his eyes felt numb. He started dancing in drag at a burlesque club downtown under the name Modest Molly Mormen. His wife divorced her. Her friends avoided her. After the cancer diagnosis, the hospital wouldn't treat her, saying she was mentally ill, so she sold her cars to pay for the Special K the dentist gave her. During one visit the cosmonaut boy told the chiropractor that one of the miracles of Jesus was curing a sick woman by putting her in a furnace. She came out of the flames a child, his fingers seemed to say. Last night, the chiropractor doused her favorite car in kerosene and, cranking up the radio, smoked a cigarette. The cosmonaut boy and the dentist watched the firemen put out the blaze. They played *Pong* on the Atari until the dentist got mad and threw the console out the window. He punched a hole in the wall. He smashed the boy's cassette tape with all the desert sounds he'd recorded. You and your stupid games, he said as his fingers started to swell, your silly ping-pong and catapults to nowhere. On Planet X we have four-dimensional baseball, the cosmonaut boy's fingers seemed to say. It's not even a real game, the dentist said, just a stupid computer code. Sometimes it's worse being with you, the cosmonaut boy's fingers seemed to say, the two of us alone together. Will you stop talking with your fingers? the dentist said, nobody understands what the hell you're saying. It's all happened before and it will all happen again, the cosmonaut boy's fingers seemed to say. Don't you get it? They want me to put you in a hospital. They think you're sick, the dentist said, tracing a finger down the space helmet along the pressure rings sutured to the boy's neck. Your fingers are broken, the cosmonaut boy's fingers seemed to say. Sometimes I wish upon a fucking star I'd never met you, the dentist said, I'd probably be happy. The cosmonaut boy's fingers seemed to say, I don't know how the cluck you people survive being happy. I can't even feel anything, the dentist said waving his gnarled fingers. He wasn't sure why he kept doing this. He didn't feel the high anymore much less crave it. The needle went in and everything was white noise. The pleasure, as best he could tell, was in waiting for it, the pretending to ignore it, the fantasizing it, the resisting it the way lovers do, and somewhere between the boot and the flush his mind was already on the next fix, that stupid gooey burning itchy deaf grim anticipation that left him soft and empty as a hardboiled egg cracked open too soon. They didn't move off the floor. The room went dark. We should go to church, the dentist said. They took turns huffing the pocket square. They listened to the firemen outside the window saying there was no suicide note left behind, but there were winning lotto scratchers in the glove box.

Jacob's Ladder

It is with sadness we communicate the passing of the cinephile, found dead in his shop yesterday lovingly holding
the severed arm prop from *The Thing from Another World*.
The first movie stub he saved was from *The She-Creature*
at the Grauman's Chinese Theatre in Los Angeles with
Maria English hypnotized and reincarnated as a prehis-
toric reptilian humanoid to do the evil bidding of a mad
scientist. It was the summer he discovered masturbation
and lived in an RV with his parents going town to town
staying in theatre parking lots and drive-ins collecting
old Hollywood memorabilia. They opened a shop downtown with the popcorn machine from the Orpheum and
the velvet ropes from the premiere of *White Zombie*. His
favorite prop was a Jacob's ladder from *Bride of Frankenstein* that sent a continuous train of electrical arcs between
two V-shaped wires. He watched monster movies over
and over, always amazed how the monster came back no
matter what. If you want to be remembered, the cinephile
told visitors, become a monster. He missed the genius of
the old horror sci-fi movies. They weren't about fantasy,
or escapism, or probing the mysteries of the human soul.
They invented breathing. The scenes making you hold
your breath, then hyperventilate, then scream your lungs
empty until you nearly pass out, movies that made your
breaths feel less satisfying once you'd gone home, less
alive, so you go back to the theatre for the next movie, the
next horror, the next fix of air. The cinephile spent a year
shooting a homemade film about a wild turkey grazing

in the Chernobyl ruins that ends up on a Thanksgiving dinner plate in Utah, the scratch from its radioactive claw infecting a father and son who—after growing waddles and feathers and beaks—zombify the town into hordes of monstrous avians who practice vegetarianism. He called it *Gobble Gobble Gorbachev*. Police found the cinephile's body last night, not long after the premiere of his movie on public access television. His face looked frustrated, as if he had no idea dying would be the most interesting thing to happen to him. For the longest time he thought things would never get better than being the Goshute County champion cherry picker when he was nine. And now I'm going places, he told customers asking for his autograph in the grocery store, I can feel it.

*Nobody says sooner or later the alien inside you says go West.
It's the pioneer sickness. Many men have it.*

*It's no coincidence that asylums and sanatoria were invented
here. The desert is a petri dish for castaways, invalids, holy fools,
nobodies. The air is thin. Time moves slow, or backwards, or
not at all.*

*Nobody watches the dust. Nobody sees the desert stretch out
like a scab some invisible hand keeps picking. Nobody sits in
a church pew and feels the dead blinking star in their head.
Nobody develops an unlimited capacity for boredom. Nobody
walks around town at night among other fathers and sons and
widowers wondering why everyone who disappears ends up in
Utah, why beautiful men die this way.*

Obit/Orbit

Died peacefully in their sleep: a divorced couple who had coffee every morning at the diner. You go too far with your friendliness, he said. Oh, she said, you talk too much to know anything about love.

Dead of asphyxiation, a hoarder crushed under the weight of his own collection. Too fat for the doorway, they had to remove him through the window. He looked like a retarded angel. Halfway through the rope snapped and his startled corpse fled the scene, tumbling down the driveway.

With the blow of an axe, a housewife cured her husband of his insomnia. Relieved, she took pills. Marriage.

An anarchist constructing a bomb in his basement paused to eat breakfast. Boiling some eggs, he burned down the house. Cause of death, according to his estranged wife, was having a stick up his ass, so the coroner, a sympathetic Mormon, put Chronic Posterior Coniferous Allergy on the certificate.

The dentist and the cosmonaut boy went to the tattoo parlor after they messed up trying to scratch some Russian words into their forearms with a paperclip. Бога нет, но это Космос. *There is no God, but there is Cosmos.* One half on the dentist's arm, the other half on the cosmonaut boy's.

A schoolgirl petitioned her mother if she could play in the yard. The mother refused, citing the weather, but the girl, who insisted she did not believe in hypothermia, played anyway. She died.

Three demonstrators dead at the protest to reopen the prophylactic distribution center. Two trampled, one of a seizure. Prayers for the fourth, visibly pregnant, hospitalized in grave condition.

Mother and daughter gave birth in the same room then died in the same room. During a somber celebration, the newborn aunt and niece passed hand-to-hand were mixed up. They will never know their true relationship.

Unpaid bills were to blame for an outage at a house next to the stockyards. Three children tried to make their own light. Pulled from the fire, their bodies were unrecognizable.

An avid bird watcher, terrified of a Russian invasion, barricaded herself in her home where, overnight, she renewed her acquaintance with carbon monoxide.

The dentist and the cosmonaut boy lay in the pickup flatbed at the drive-in watching a double feature of *The Day the Earth Stood Still* and *The Magnetic Monster*. Out of curiosity, what happened here? the dentist asked, tracing his finger along the crack in the space helmet. Out of curiosity, the cosmonaut boy's fingers seemed to say.

A certain chef rushed into the hotel room and fired six shots at his wife and her lover. They all missed. After the two men slugged each other unconscious, the wife looked around for two more bullets. Over a fry sauce recipe, the police say, not romance.

Children played games with a corpse lying in the alfalfa field. His face was picked clean by a parliament of owls. They thought he was a scarecrow.

The divorcee refused alimony. Finding this arrangement too agreeable, her estranged husband strangled her.

Efforts to rescue an amateur spelunker trapped in the hydrothermal caves did not go smoothly. Exhausted by their failures, rescuers accused the spelunker of not trying hard enough to be saved. After a brief rest, he slipped through the crevasse and fell, presumably, to his death.

The cosmonaut boy's fingers wondered if there would be girls on Planet X like the *Orgy of the Dead*. Wishing is for suckers, the dentist told him, pointing at a shooting star as the last of green Jell-O dissolved on his tongue like magic, as if he'd eaten nothing at all and so he went back for more and it dissolved again without a trace, almost like there was something otherworldly about Jell-O and the cosmonaut boy's fingers seemed to say, I think I was born in the wrong time. Do you think there's religion on your planet? the dentist asked. I'm going to miss Jell-O, the cosmonaut boy's fingers seemed to say, it's the only proof there might be a God. Maybe we'll always be relapsing Mormons, the dentist said. The voice of God is bewilderness, the cosmonaut boy's fingers seemed to say, there's no getting clean from it.

Denied charity from the church, a septuagenarian, winner of the meningitis lottery, died a slow, painful death. His children watched, doing everything they could to slow the process.

Black mold in the walls, not syphilis, killed the bartender. His body sat in his room nine days. Famished, his beloved dog ate his face, then leapt out the window with entrails in tow, then into the fog and was seen no more.

With the gas leak catastrophe averted, relieved tenants returned to their apartments and took to celebrating. One dead from a drinking game, another after falling from the balcony, and a child, unrelated, who succumbed after eating scores of fat pickles.

Feverish, the banker, an old friend of chlamydia, was knifed by prostitutes across the street from the meatpacking factory. Trying to stop the bleeding, one of the more kind-hearted girls plugged his wounds with a bullet. Modern medicine.

A case of unrequited love. The poet, out on the pond in his rowboat, tried to kiss the moon's reflection. Drowned.

God's closing the fridge, the cosmonaut boy's fingers seemed to say. The sky went dark. He pointed at the flickering stars. The dentist said if he was being honest he really hated the stars, or maybe he was just frustrated they were so far away, like big alien eyes winking as if they knew some secret or were playing a trick on us, like maybe God poured them into the sky one ladle at a time and expects someone else to mop up the mess. The cosmonaut boy's fingers seemed to say, I live in stars.

To relieve their rheumatism, two church ladies bathed at the spa in melted whale blubber. After six hours, one lady was cured. The other suffocated on the fumes and was pronounced healed but dead.

Capricious winds knocked down power lines across the city. A girl thought one looked like a jump rope. She could not be revived even after several anointings with consecrated oil.

Somebody kept interfering with the farmer's goats. He shot the perpetrator, then milked the goats before putting them down. Barbeque tomorrow, all are welcome.

Two sisters dead after falling from the water tower where they were graffitiing. THE TOWN WHERE LOVE PREVAILS AND GOD SURVEILS. Their mother, unlucky with love, is pregnant with another.

By the time the doctor phoned to correct the error, the dishwasher had made peace with his diagnosis and was cocktailed with morphine and bleach. He loved life, just not his own.

They climbed the water tower where the cosmonaut boy used a penknife to carve a poem into the wood: *Here I could pluck the stars/ with my hand. I dare not speak aloud/ in the silence. For fear/ of disturbing the dwellers of heaven.*

A woman laughing in her sleep was shushed by her husband. Unaware, she bit his finger. Dead two weeks later, blood poisoning.

The thief, his son, and his pious wife. Dead after drinking the milk of a tubercular cow. Whereabouts currently unknown.

A young woman of the night defended her virtue against accusations she used scissors to deprive the victim of his virility. It's well known, she said at trial, that all the whores in town are well-behaved.

Two paperboys dead at the grocery store on Newton Street. Over roast beef sandwiches, not a girl.

Coming down the playground slide, a boy, almost 3, was impaled through the mouth with a hobbyhorse. The mother, a community theatre actress, has nine others to feed.

They went to the Malt Shoppe and the dentist watched the cosmonaut boy pour six milkshakes down the oxygen hose. The dentist said that wasn't going to help him run around the baseball diamond, and the cosmonaut boy's fingers seemed to say the secret alien hiding among humans in the old sci-fi movies is always the quiet one, the one who never says anything, like they know better than to trust words. The dentist slid a cassette tape across the table. I tried to get all the same sounds as before, the dentist said. Wind and sand and stars, he smiled. It's quiet in outer space, the dentist said, you might want to hear home.

The construction worker showed his co-workers the thirty-six milky scars he'd notched on his arm. One for every liaison. More or less melancholic while carving number thirty-seven, he nicked an artery and bled out.

A colored boy living in a HUD house hoping to get enough money to fund his country music album robbed the post office. Arriving at the scene, police officers ordered the boy, then missing two fingers, to put his hands into the air. They shot him fourteen times. He was reaching for something, authorities insisted.

I left here once, the dentist said. Away from the desert, away from the dust and sun and lizards and salt and all these Mormons who knew me down to the bones and knew the bones of my bones, and would you believe it, I felt a little empty. I'd rather throw a no-hitter than hit a walk-off homerun, the cosmonaut boy's sticky milkshake fingers seemed to say. I couldn't cope in the city, the dentist said. Maybe it was too normal, or maybe I needed to be in a place that was dreamt and not actually real. Pitching is the closest thing there is to God, the cosmonaut boy's fingers seemed to say. Nobody gets to hold onto who they are for very long, the dentist said. You get old. If you're lucky you forget. The pitcher is the only artist out there, the cosmonaut boy's fingers seemed to say, the rest are just mathematicians. But most just breathe out everything they are every minute of their life, the dentist said, everyone on borrowed air. The cosmonaut boy's fingers seemed to say, A pitch after a pitch after a pitch is a gospel. I can't imagine how difficult it is for you out here, the dentist said. If it were me, the cosmonaut boy's fingers seemed to say, I would only throw knuckleballs. That's the pitch not even God can hit.

Stirred by compassion, the neighborhood sent dozens of flower arrangements to the widower. He put them in the bed, hoping to disguise the imprint his wife of sixty years left on the mattress. Pollen, not grief, killed him.

After failing to kill his sister, who was following the recipe directions differently than their mother, the cashier, who fancied himself a philosopher, put his head in the oven. Well done.

A stone mason working on theatre renovations lost his footing and fell headfirst off the scaffolding into, as luck would have it, an industrial cement mixer. It was the widow's third husband. Unlike the previous, he had a thick skull and lukewarm heart.

They swam in the creek. They ate soggy bologna sandwiches on white bread stuffed with potato chips. Back at the capsule, they oiled the bike chain and put a fresh coat of lacquer on the nautical helm. They scavenged a new antenna for the ham radio in the landfill. They checked the catapult counterweights and made sure the rope was taught. The dentist said it wouldn't work. He said it wasn't safe and they should find more cantaloupe for practice tests. The cosmonaut boy's fingers seemed to say, All my life I've been drowning in this desert, not one fucking drop of water in sight, but I've been drowning, and this town just complains I smell fishy. Be grateful you can't talk, the dentist said, shaking his head at the dust devils. Look at this place. Everyone lost for words in a world where nothing matters except words.

A man, stricken seventy years with digestive distress, could only use the toilet while at church after an inspiring sermon. He lost his faith, and then his life. Bowel obstruction.

A pistol accidentally discharged during a sacrament service at the local chapel. Two suspects. Three witnesses. Thoughts and prayers for the victim.

Two hunters felled a bear. Posing for photos, the beast revived and mauled them accordingly.

Nothing to see here, authorities said as they removed the body overdosed in the alley. A clumsy onlooker, trying to get a better view, fell from the roof and cracked his skull. Dead at the scene.

Dead from poisoning, a husband who for thirty-two years had pretended to be deaf so as to not have to talk with his wife. No sooner had his wife learned sign language than the husband began complaining of vision problems. Deafness is tolerable, the wife confessed to the authorities, but a blind man is too much.

When he asked, Which one is your home? the dentist watched the cosmonaut boy trace his finger along the empty spaces of the constellation map. The movie in my head doesn't play home any more, his fingers seemed to say. He held the map to the sky. It looks lonely up there, the dentist said. The boy's fingers seemed to say, It's lonely down here.

A thousand miles from the sea, the Sunday school teacher, a former sailor, bludgeoned his children with an antique whale flensing blade. Boredom, he said.

A woman, who believed her stillborn child was reincarnated as radio static, brought the device to the bishop hoping he would baptize it and save the child's soul. That's perverse, the bishop said. The loving mother plugged in the radio and baptized the two of them in the tub.

The serial hugger has struck again, this time in the HUD neighborhood. He embraced a man waiting for the bus, causing the latter to hyperventilate until he had no more breaths to give. Authorities will not say if these are crimes of passion.

Twenty-three children went under their desks for the fallout drill. Two, wild mushroom connoisseurs during recess, did not return.

The psychiatrist fell down a manhole and was injured. Recovering, he crossed the street and was hit by a car, injured once more. Pausing under an awning, he was electrocuted and, closing his eyes, this time did not wake up.

The secretary, obsessed with crossword puzzles, was knifed in the alley behind the psychic shop at the hands of parties unknown. The bishop ignored her request for a blessing. She died.

This is my church, the cosmonaut boy's fingers seemed to say as he traced fingers over the capsule. The dentist asked if he would take off the space helmet, just this once? The cosmonaut boy's fingers seemed to say, Nobody can live like this. I'm sorry, the dentist said, I still don't understand.

The peeper was loitering outside the window when a couple returned to their home, so the husband clubbed him with a nearby flowerpot. He was found hours later, two streets away, bleeding from the wound. Sleepwalking, he lied, then said no more.

Exacerbated, a husband tried convincing his wife his mistress was not a mistress but a wife from a different life, just as she had been his wife in other lives too. She shot him out of religious doubt, not jealousy.

A humorless liberal was run over by an ambulance while jaywalking. Gone too soon, the wife said. Alive too long, the neighbors said.

Having hiccupped steadily for eleven years, a woman committed herself to the State Hospital. The hiccups ceased unexpectedly. Unsure who she was anymore, the woman transferred from the hospital to the cemetery.

A professor persisted in complaining about his wife's expensive cooking. She knocked out his teeth with a hammer. Cooking doesn't agree with me, she told the judge, I don't like to stir, and then persuaded him to pass a lesser sentence because she was more frugal than cruel.

The dentist traced a baseball diamond in the salt flats with his foot. At the four corners he put copies of the Book of Mormon. If I can strike you out, he said, then you have to stay. But if you score, you can go back to Planet X. The boy fouled off pitches with the wok. It was getting dark. He laced a curveball that ricocheted off the dentist's head out into the salt flats. It was a race to home plate. The dentist dove. The cosmonaut boy slid. When the dentist looked up he saw the cosmonaut boy sprawled out and flipping him the bird. Nobody said anything.

It's true that a housewife on Templeton Street was sane when she married the man she now believes to be a Russian spy. Yesterday, she pushed the stroller in front of the bus while her husband, fond of the choir, was at church.

Exposed as an embezzler of church tithes, again, the comptroller shot himself. His brains traveled a good distance while his heart kept still. Story of his life.

Workers digging new telephone lines happened upon the skeletons of four infants. City improvements will be delayed.

A man with a head tucked under his arm like a bowling ball was apprehended downtown insisting he had been desperately trying to reunite the head with the body for several hours. The jury found such testimony implausible until the man admitted he was a devout patriarch in the local congregation and eighth generation Mormon of good pioneer stock, at which point they agreed with his reasoning that the woman, his wife of thirty-seven years, might still be alive had she been as compassionate and docile as a wife as she was a head.

The dentist helped the cosmonaut boy into the silky underwear spacesuit and told him how when you go to the Mormon temple you get a new name, the cosmic name that was yours before coming to this world, the real name you've just forgotten, and promise never to tell anyone this name or else your throat will be cut ear to ear and your tongue torn out by its roots. The dentist said he'd never told anyone his new name, not even his wife, and he'd lived so long in this faithsick place he wasn't sure he could tell the cosmonaut boy his name even now, because when he was a boy everyone told him he was destined for spiritual greatness, but look at me, he said, I'm nobody. You promise not to tell anyone? the dentist said. He put his lips to the cracked helmet and whispered.

The penny stock trader dragged his crippled grandfather down the street on a soiled mattress before heaving both the old man and the mattress into the river. The grandfather, crawling out of the water on two suddenly sturdy legs, complained he was going to catch pneumonia. The penny stock trader waited for his grandfather to climb back up the embankment, then threw him in again.

Heated with gin and love, a bridesmaid tried to rekindle her affections with the groom. He refused. She sabotaged the marriage anyway.

Bit by a raccoon three weeks ago, a child suffering from rabies was baptized a second time. It had zero effect.

Charged with corrupting the innocence of a minor, the judge a month away from his pension carved PIG into his stomach then hurled himself into the quarry. Divers found two bodies, but not the one they're looking for.

Aroused with ire that she had been cheated out of an inheritance, a geriatric drove her car into the family ice cream parlor downtown. A customer went into premature labor. Fire engulfed the building. Nostalgicide, infanticide, urbicide.

Pedal hard or there won't be enough escape velocity and you'll get stuck in orbit, the dentist said. Half-smiling he said, Just don't get yourself killed. The cosmonaut boy's fingers seemed to say, There are lots of ways to ghost. He fastened the parachute. He flipped the ham radio switch. The static crackled.

A brotherhood of knights from the KKK arrived from Salt Lake hoping to recruit new members. Touring Calypsee, a few of the local church elders treated them to good Caucasian fun white-water rafting. They drowned.

In time for the holidays: a former beauty queen weighed down with rocks surfaced in the quarry. Her father confessed to the murder. For being a fool, not an ingrate.

A housewife was on the phone with friends and family sharing the good news when she died by mistake. Her hobbies were soap carving, gardening, jujitsu.

Inside the abandoned van found in the desert was a fever dream. Migrant women and children packed tight and pickled like herring. No arrests expected.

Squatters refused to leave the house of the county executive. Unsatisfied with his legal options, he burned the house down. The smoke was visible for miles.

The dentist reminded the boy the catapult wasn't safe to launch. The cosmonaut boy tapped his watch and pointed to the sky. With a finger, he drew little circles in the dust. I don't know what that is, the dentist said, you could be drawing a cosmic chicken for all I know. The cosmonaut boy's fingers seemed to say, Syzygy. The dentist said something could go wrong. He knew it was silly but wondered if they should say a prayer. The cosmonaut boy laced up his boots and his fingers seemed to say as he nodded at his drawing in the dust, Nobody's a traveler of time and space.

His car impounded the night before, the drunk arrived at the bar on his lawnmower which was quickly towed away. The following night he arrived atop his cow, only to see it butchered and barbecued. Spreading out the cowhide, the drunk rafted down the street and into a snow drift where he was discovered the next morning dead of hypothermia.

Fearing her friendliness had become burdensome, a poor woman working three part-time jobs smothered her baby with a pillow. The prosecutor, a paragon of compassion on Sundays, is seeking the death penalty. Firing squad.

Seduced by a farrago of truth and dream, a schoolboy fell down the mine shaft in search of the old salt city. Ninth this year.

A man continued his efforts to relieve our town of its whiteness by disposing items into the landfill: piano keys, snow, cauliflower, cotton underwear, wedding dresses, chalk, vanilla ice cream, baseballs, aspirin, milk, toilet paper, mayonnaise, daffodils, fingernails, salt, teeth, sheep, ducks, sugar, daisies, rice, coconuts, phone books, eggs, bones, and a not insignificant variety of cheeses. With only the clouds eluding him, he walked everywhere with aerosol cans spraying a chemical of his own invention that tickled the nose and left a sour taste in the mouth. Yesterday, he fell from a hot-air balloon and very nearly survived.

It's hot, the dentist said rubbing his sunburnt neck. What if you came with me? the cosmonaut boy's fingers seemed to say. The desert stretched on and on in a murmuring shade of white. You probably don't want me to, but I'd go with you only I'm too old, and it's too late for me, the dentist said. Then the cosmonaut boy's fingers seemed to say the ice city where he was from melted during the day but at night the water droplets refroze, rising like pale dreamy stalagmites and tessellating into glacial skyscrapers and crystalized spires. You talk too much, the dentist said. It's cold there, the cosmonaut boy's fingers seemed to say, but heaven is always sad.

A case of revenge. A woman, crazed as a bedbug, pushed a piano off the balcony, crushing her lover. They were married yesterday.

A woman taken into custody last night on suspicion of drowning her quintuplets claims it is a case of mistaken identity as she cannot be the mother because her children are changelings.

Beating his wife was more exertion than the math teacher, a devout Mormon of good pioneer stock, could bear. He suffered a burst appendix. Justice.

The mechanic and the school groundskeeper, neighbors, disputed who must rake the leaves from the tree that split the property. The mechanic lifted a spade, the groundskeeper a hedge clipper. And so the issue was resolved.

I'm a little bit upset by the fact that you're real, the dentist said. I don't know if you figured it out yet, but I can't live without imaginary things. So, you being real is a bit of a disappointment. Nobody cares, the cosmonaut boy's fingers seemed to say. You were out, the dentist said, handing the boy the wok. The cosmonaut boy handed the scuffed baseball to the dentist. They closed the hatch.

A man who recorded his voice at the so-called voicebank for deaf mutes and those who have, through accident or biological error, lost the use of their natural voice and who can, with the assistance of a machine speak using one of the donated voices, immediately stopped talking after his donation. He wrote it was unnatural for one voice to occupy two spaces. When his recorded voice became the most popular selection at the voicebank, preferred by hundreds of mute strangers who sent him gratitude cards almost daily, he burned down the voicebank with himself inside it, leaving those who still use his mechanical voice to wonder if they too are insane.

It was a unanimous vanity that compelled a graphic designer to beat to death with a tire iron a child as he walked home yesterday. He informed authorities he came from a family of printers and had spent the last five decades investing all his inheritance, accumulating thousands in debt and bankrupting his business, trying to create a new typeface which he hoped would leave a lasting legacy in the publishing world, only to see his work ignored and, eventually, replaced by a computer program. He killed the child, he confessed, hoping to see his name in the newspaper using his original typeface, if only this once.

The dentist greased the channel before inspecting the pivots and counterweights. He tightened the axle nuts one last time. He checked his watch. He rubbed his foot in the dust, erasing the cosmonaut boy's circles. He gazed at the stars, looking for the syzygy. He closed his eyes and pulled the lever. The trebuchet wobbled as the rope hissed and the wooden arm swung with a loud groan.

Deceased overnight, the bishop who announced from the pulpit that, henceforth, those deceased in the faith require a permit to resurrect in the afterlife and that all resurrections performed without the necessary paperwork and accompanying signatures—one from an authorized ecclesiastical official and one from the State Council of Religious Affairs—were null and void and of no efficacy, and that permits issued by non-Mormon institutions, naturally, were automatically disqualified. His passing is full of mystery and murmurs.

A child, burned in a propane explosion over 90% of his body, woke up long enough to ask if there were peanut butter and jelly sandwiches in heaven. Then he died.

Nobody saw what happened. The capsule soared into outer space. It drifted a few hundred yards then crash-landed. It never launched at all. Nobody knows. Only that when the dentist opened the hatch, the boy was gone.

He said in the morning he found a jagged line of footprints in the salt flats. The scientists said those were fossilized from the Ice Age, briefly visible after it rained until the sun dried them out and they disappeared again, but nobody really knows.

The trebuchet is still there. The wood splintered, the bolts rusty, the rope frayed. Travelers lost along the highway either looking for a gas station or the way to Los Angeles often pull off the road to pore over maps and wonder what the medieval-looking thing is and ask the old man pacing in circles where they are, the old man with shaggy white hair who opens and closes the capsule hatch and says it smells like orchids, showing them the brittle petals he once found inside, the old man drinking milk from a carton with the cosmonaut boy's space helmet face on the side—HAVE YOU SEEN ME?—who goes back to searching the skies with his binoculars, waving the baseball at the travelers when they ask what's that city beyond the salt flats because who in God's name would want to live out here? Nobody, the old man says, as the travelers hurry back to their cars and drive off into the desert, that's nobody's city.

Acknowledgements

Every book is the illegitimate love child of other books. I am grateful to the writers—living, dead, or otherwise—I was reading, teaching, and thinking about while drafting this book over nineteen years, and whose words influenced, inspired, and shaped my own, and from whom I borrowed, stole, and imitated by degrees: Thomas Bernhard, Paul la Farge, John Steinbeck, Miguel de Cervantes, Viktor Pelevin, J. Robert Lennon, Lydia Davis, Edward Abbey, Wallace Stenger, Michael Martone, Rabelais, Brian Evenson, W.G. Sebald, Jan Potocki, J.M Tyree, Dubravka Ugrešić, Li Bai, and Felix Fénéon.

My gratitude to the literary journals who published excerpts: *Booth, Conjunctions, Puerto del Sol, 100-Word Story, Tupelo Quarterly, Atticus Review, hex literary,* and *Denver Quarterly.* And to Scott Zieher who exhibited photos and obituaries at the ZieherSmith Gallery in Nashville. A special thanks to Rob Stapleton who didn't hesitate to debut this project and breathe life into it when I was too afraid to show it to anyone. Another special thanks to my old friend, Laura Hurtado—tallest sister in the family— who gave many of these necronauts an unexpected home in the Utah Museum of Contemporary Art.

Thanks to Scott W. Berg, Bodie Fox, Jacob Sharp, Taylor Schaefer, Paul Logan, Camille Koslo, and everyone at Stillhouse Press who not only designed a beautiful book and gave it such a wonderful home, but worked tirelessly to get it into readers' hands. Thanks to Salisbury University for the sabbatical that allowed me time to wander the Great Basin and Mojave Desert so I could finish the manuscript.

And for Jenna, always, my witty alien co-pilot who makes this strange cosmic ride worthwhile.

The Author

Ryan Habermeyer is the author of the short story collections *Salt Folk* and *The Science of Lost Futures*. His award-winning stories and essays have appeared in *Conjunctions*, *Alaska Quarterly Review*, *Copper Nickel*, *Massachusetts Review*, *DIAGRAM* and others. A Fulbright Scholar who has lived, studied, and taught in Poland, Scotland, Spain, and Mexico, he is Associate Professor of Creative Writing at Salisbury University in Maryland.

www.ingramcontent.com/pod-product-compliance
Lightning Source LLC
Chambersburg PA
CBHW020911060726
47591CB00004B/1181